The Chronometer

By

Terry T. Turner

I first would like to thank God almighty for blessing me with such a vastly overactive imagination. Secondly I'm thankful for my stubborn mindset that allows me to continue down the path less traveled no matter how long it takes.

Patience is a virtue.

Sara, I'm so thankful for your unconditional love and enduring strength when it comes to me. I know I'm not easiest one to be with sometimes, especially when I'm lost in thought which seems like it's all the time.

Mom & Dad thank you so much for always believing in me and being there for me, your advice and guidance has made me the man I am today. I love you both more than you know.

Morgan my little girl, you are the most amazing story I could ever create. Thank you for always finding the best in your grumpy ole Dad. I love you with all my heart.

Last but not least I want to thank my fans. I truly don't know how you all found my stories but I'm thankful you did. There's nothing better than writing to please myself and finding out I'm not the only one out there that enjoys these tales.

Contents

Prologue

In the Blink

Of an

Eye

It's well past a young boy's bedtime as he sits at the edge of his bed watching the lightning flash across the sky and for a split second igniting his room in a ball of light. The thunderstorm rages on outside as the exhausted boy scans the ground in between the flashes watching for any signs of life out in the darkness.

The man he's searching for out in the torrential rain is his estranged father who he's never met though his mom promised he'd see him again one rainy day. So every time the rain comes in Oliver Pendulum can't help but to pray he sees his dad for the first time as he dozes off to sleep while fighting it the whole way. …

Oliver is startled out of his slumber by a ruckus downstairs when a blood curdling scream cuts through the night. Frightened at his mom's screaming that just went silent with a snap Oliver scurries over to his go to hiding spot trying to stay out of sight from the heavy footsteps that sound like they're headed his way.

Ollie could sense evil on the other side of the door and watches with tears in his eyes as the doorknob slowly turns. A sudden noise down stairs causes the knob to quickly spring back and Ollie feels the evil presence vanish in the blink of an eye as he hears a man furiously shouting out in rage, "Corvan I'm going to kill you! Do you hear me, you're dead! This is the last time you take my love from ME!"

The stairs let out an eerie creek breaking the long silence after the violent decree on the ground floor. Ollie again feels the presence of someone at his door when suddenly the man on the other side crashes through running into the wall in the process.

"Who are you?" Ollie asks causing the man who's now franticly rummaging through Ollie's closet slinging clothes and shoes out as fast as he can to stop and take pause from what he's doing. It's been so long, the last time the man had seen his son was on the day of Oliver's birth.

"My official name is Bartholomew Wallace Pendulum but you can call me Dad." Bart says as he gathers up the clothes gently placing them in the small suitcase he found under the bed.

"We have to go now and I need you to trust me." Bart tells his son who looks willing to believe but reserved in his response.

"How do I know you're really my dad? I mean I've never even seen my dad." Ollie states bringing a smile to the face of his supposed dad who thinks out loud.

"Your Mother taught you well. I bet she told you about me and my fancy little timepiece here hasn't she." Bart says with a smile as he pulls up his sleeve reviling the mythical time device his son had heard so much about. Ollie's mom use to tell him all about the chronometer and all the amazing things she witnessed it do.

Bart sees the smile fight through the fear on Ollie's face as his son remembers all the extraordinary tales his mother told him about his adventuring dad, how much he loved Ollie and the reason that his dad left was to protect them from an evil monster.

"Come on boy it's time to go." Bart says with a smile putting Ollie's coat on him and guiding him out under the safety of his arm.

"Where are we going?" Ollie gets the gumption up to ask as all the questions he's ever had about his dad fight to all come out at once.

"On a train ride." ...

Chapter One

The Unvanished

It's the end of an Era.

The year is 1979.

The place is the Abnormal Studies class on the campus of Berkley. …

She slips in unnoticed to all but her most trusted old professor who gives a slight grin to one of his favorite graduates who still retains her punctuality from her days as his student before setting her out for being late, "Brinly Rachel Blevins, on time as always I see. Class this is the infamous BRB I'm sure you've heard all about her. She's a true legend of our time."

Brinly sheepishly stands and waves to the nearly full classroom before retaking her seat ready to hear the professor's tale of the day. She's waiting till the class is over to pick her old professors' brain. Brinly pulls out an old spiral notebook ready to add some notes to her 'who is the Unvanished' book. Brinly has continued to search for the answer to the question that's driven her since she was a little kid, which is written on the front of her old and tattered journal.

Brinly grew up in the suburbs with two parents who loved her dearly. After all she was their little miracle. She never had any reason to doubt that her father worked in the financial district and eked out a very nice living for himself and his little family though sometimes he was gone for long patches of Brinly's childhood. Her mother said he was a prized speaker for the firm of Jackson, Wolf, & Associates and that they should be proud of him. She filled the void like only a mother could playing the role of Susie homemaker to the tee, never letting on that there could be more to her than just a happy housewife.

When it was just the two of them her mother used to tell Brinly fantastic stories about the Unvanished and where he could be today? Then some days she told other stories about those who sought him out though she never called them anything other than the secret people.

Then there were the tales Brinly's father told her about a hero named Jack whenever he was home from his trips. Brinly would sit in her Dad's lap while he read the paper. Brinly's dad always liked to pretend that he was reading the stories right off the page when in fact they were much closer to the reality he's lived in secret his whole life. He'd dare not reveal he's actually a Agent of the Jacks fearing the truth to be too dangerous for his little miracle of a family.

Brinly can thank those unique and extraordinary stories from both sides of her family tree for being the sole reason she went into the field she did. It's safe to say cults and secret societies are Brinly's passion. And after college she picked up her dream job freelancing as a tracker of the mystical for the same logistics firm her Dad retired from. The pay is good but the work is what drives her. Brinly loves the chase.

Brinly chuckles as the professor clears his throat before restarting the mysterious tale of the Unvanished to his class with the instructions for them to look for the answer as to what happened.

"This is taken from the Sacramento Tribune. The date was October 18th 1892, I hope you enjoy. ...

Sometime late in the night two nights ago there was an unexplainable catastrophe at the train station rendering the locomotive and six of the cars in total ruins along with the collapse of the depot and the tracks under the train. Deputy Jones was the first on the scene describing it as like nothing he'd ever seen before. The structures damage consisted of the wood planks turned to stone, the iron nails turned to rust. But the locomotive, the brand new locomotive that had just arrived at the station now looks like it was made of wood eat up with termites. The boiler is tilted back with the base actually resting in the dirt with the cab leaning forward resting in the same spot giving the locomotive a V-shaped outline. Those who were in the cars further back explained that there was a sudden burst of light and an alarming quake that echoed through the rest of the train. ..."

Professor Giest pauses only momentarily for suspense before continuing, "This class, is where it gets interesting because standing in the dead center of the blast was a single child. He looked to be about nine or ten at the time of the photograph. He was wrapped up in a grown up's coat with a lost expression on his face. You can tell by his expression that he has no idea as to how to handle what it was he just saw... What was it he saw?" Professor Giest explains ending with an unanswerable question as the projector casts the only known image of the accident ever recorded upon the screen.

The image shows a young boy holding a large coat around him by the collar as he stands in the center of where the blast came from. The class quietly focuses on the picture knowing the professor will have some kind of pop quiz about it at the end of his lecture.

"Miraculously he is unharmed unlike the growing list of missing passengers that had quarters in the front six cars. We called him the Unvanished since he was the only one who didn't disappear in the accident though soon after the photograph was taken he went missing. Of course there were always rumored sightings of the boy but never any proof he ever existed to begin with. Well that is except for th..." "…That photo is FAKE!" Professor Giest is interrupted from a student eager for knowledge. So he pauses to take a drink wetting his pallet before bringing it home with his zinger of the answer to his current know-it-alls outburst.

The comment was yelled from a small group at the top left of the auditorium style classroom causing the class to erupt into an ocean of arguments and shouts of conjecture.

"Quiet down, quiet down, everyone settle down." The professor says as he drops an impossibly large book on the floor. The impact of the giant book sends a shocked look of panic through the arguing classmates giving Professor Giest the floor once again.

"Stand up great debater, let yourself be seen." the professor calmly asks and waits till a brash young man stands up with a smirk on his face as he jovially smacked his buddies shoulder while getting up.

"So genius, tell us how you miraculously figured out that this photo is a fake from? What row is that exactly? I can't tell from this far away." Professor Giest sarcastically asks this obvious smartass trying to look cool in front of his friends.

Undeterred the young man gives a quick chuckle before pointing at the one of a kind timepiece loosely hanging on the boy's exposed forearm. "The watch is all the proof you need. Look at it, that's obviously not of that time period. And if that's not real then the pictures not real i.e. it has to be a fake."

A gleaming smile grows across Professor Giest face as he seems genuinely impressed by the young punk's observation. "I'm impressed you noticed the timepiece, many have lost their lives in search of it, isn't it beautiful. You'll never find its equal and oh how I wish it were mine." the professor says as he gives a longing glance at the watch before rejoining the group.

"Believe it or not this photo has been authenticated by professors in this very university as the genuine article, so that now leaves the question of who is the boy and where is the chronometer? Because 87 years after the tragic accident that miraculous device has yet to be found. The running theory is that the chronometer and its wearer are still out there roaming the earth." Professor Giest says as his alarm goes off indicating that time is up.

"Alright class theories on the desk by this time tomorrow include where you think the chronometer could be using all the rumored sightings we've discussed, be sure to get your rest this weekend cause next week its what you've all been waiting for, The Jacks are coming the Jacks are coming." Giest shouts to his curious class who's packing up and starting to exit the lecture hall most engaged in conversation on the topic of the day while a student lingers behind the rest of his friends to ask about a rumor he had heard.

"Sir is it true you give extra credit for any real evidence of those Happy Jacks you mentioned?" the young man asks with more concern garnered over the grades than the very dangerous information he appears to have.

Professor Giest takes a moment as he reflects on how the young man phrased his question before answering with slight frown. "I'm sorry but it's not school policy to risk a student's life in the pursuit of knowledge." Giest says the protocol answer with a wink and a nod of his head in an agreeing manner about the info.

The confusing answer the young man receives causes him to slowly walk away while still processing what it was the professor actually said. "Interesting?" Professor Giest softly says as he watches the young man pocket what looks like a very shiny dog whistle.

"So how was the trip, did you see anything spooky this time?" Giest turns and asks as he puts on his coat grabbing his briefcase while leading Brinly out of his classroom once his students had left the room.

"Nothing too crazy with the group, no real threats just a bunch of wishful thinkers. That's why I'm here. I need to pick your brain." Brinly says with a little disappointment on not finding an amazing pot of gold at the end of the rainbow so to speak.

"Really I find that hard to believe? You need help finding the macabre." the Professor says with a smile before adding, "And how's your pet project going, any new clues on the Unvanished?"

"It's a rabbit hole that just keeps on going, I'm not sure I'm searching for a real person at this point, just a rumor." Brinly says with a sigh having a moment of doubt about the mystery she's chased her whole life.

"I wish I could just go back to catching Jacks and stop obsessing over a myth." Brinly says with a shrug.

"Did you ever catch a Jack?" Giest asks with his eyebrow raised and a grin growing on his face knowing the comment will dig a little deeper with his pupil than he intended.

"Low blow professor, low blow, you know I would've had him if it weren't for the... well you know I had one cornered. It was just that the wolves wanted him more." Brinly says with a scornful look at the professor for bringing up such a traumatic event in her life. She nearly died that night and to this day she can't remember exactly how she escaped only that she dreamed a monster saved her from the wolves.

"I know I'm sorry for mentioning it. But believe me the answer is out there, he's out there somewhere, so have a little faith. You never know you may run into him while getting your morning coffee, but are more likely to find him at a bar." Giest says as he smiles at Brinly like a proud poppa.

"That's asking a lot from someone like me." Brinly says as she leans up against the professor's vintage piece of art dedicated to the automotive world's finest racers. It's not that she doesn't have faith it's more of which one to have faith in regards to her ideology.

"So I've been tracking this group for what feels like an eternity and I'm finally on the cusp of my first real glimpse of its inner workings... What do you know about the Followers... or the..." Brinly says reminding the Professor of why she's here when he interrupts.

"Followers of the Guise." Professor Giest announces with a touch of pride in his voice for the unknown group of religious fanatics.

"Yes! I knew you'd have something solid for me! All I've come up with are myth and rumor... You know I always loved how this thing first sounds when you fire it up." Brinly says as she pushes off the front fender to a new position beside the driver's door while opening her own door.

"Go home get some rest I'll call you tomorrow, get something set in stone." Giest says as he draws Brinly's full interest.

"You got a lead on something?" Brinly perks up with excitement, "You might as well tell me now, I won't be able to sleep till I know."

"Ok, ok, I've heard about a curious cult sighting, there's very little known of this group it might just be the Followers you're after? They're having a welcoming party for new members' on Saturday night. Rumor is they're loyal to the Guise, I bet you'll find your answer there." Giest says with a smirk like he knew something she didn't. He hands Brinly a file knowing this will just keep her up the rest of the night. Brinly is overwhelmed with joy about a new assignment quickly glancing through the small list of names and profiles not seeing an address.

"I'm on it Boss, you got an address for me?" Brinly says as she cracks the door open on her own ride before adding, "How do I get in?"

"Go to 5020 Cypress Lane and then take the gravel driveway just past the house. Oh that's in Paradise so pack a lunch for the ride up, tell them you dreamt of the address, believe it or not that'll get you in. Oh and Brinly...

Try to be careful this time." Giest says with a smile knowing there's no stopping her once the intrigue sets in which is exactly the reason he sent her on this task. …

In the Midwest near the more lo-key end of Chicago at the mysterious 'Jackson, Wolf, and Associates' we find Ollie walking through the front doors of a large and extravagantly well funded private practice for doctors in the old location of the once infamous 'Murder Castle' though you wouldn't recognize it today. Mainly due to the fact that the Jacks tore down the building re-erecting a much larger building on top of what's hid beneath.

The Murder Castle was a three story house of horrors built in the early 1890's by the infamous H.H. Holmes, and yes he was a Jack. There's several floors hid from the world's view under the building. It was rumored he built all the secret passages and trap doors to prey upon the public and tourists swarming the city for the 1893 World's Fair and there's probably some truth to that, Holmes so loved to extinguish life.

But the real reason the structure was built was to combat the worst kinds of evil. And as the old saying goes the best way to fight monsters is with monsters of your own. Man always takes the cake when you discuss their violent nature to destroy everything around them, making them the perfect hunters for monsters.

Ollie twists the dial on his watch manipulating the time stream causing him to disappear right in front of the check-in with none the wiser of his actions.

It's only moments later that Ollie reappears on the fifth floor with his watch set to keep him out of sight of the men and women going about their daily work routines, but to him they look like statues due to his manipulation in time. Ollie continues on his path and as he passes the different offices he hears a lot of the same questions and wonders if the patients/victims ever notice the guise.

Truth is it's not a Doctor's office at all, that's just the cover used by the little known yet very powerful society nicknamed *the Happy Jacks*. Their most famous Jack being that of the murderous Jack the Ripper, you see there is a little known fact about those terrible crimes nobody in the sane world knows about.

That fact being that those poor women had a rare disease known as lycanthropy, which if you believe in that type of thing you can see where he was trying to protect his fellow humans from the wolves.

But if you don't believe in ghosts, werewolves, and monsters under the bed, then it just seems like mass murder. In fact it was mass murder, something the Jacks have been doing for centuries.

The Jacks work outside of the realm of what's legal or more in fact they work outside the realm of what's real. And depending on which side of the line you stand on when you face them decides whether you they're friend or foe, the latter comes' with grave consequence to all who try and appose them. The Jacks have set their sights on the supernatural side of the world with eradication the goal. But once you've gotten a taste for it, who knows where it will end?

Ollie hates being here. He's never been a fan of their practices having a run in with the Jacks a long time ago which left its mark and has kept Ollie away from this place except for the rarest of occasions, today just happens to be that kind of day.

"But today somebody owes me a favor." he thinks to himself as he stops at his destination which is an ear shot from the doctor inside who's having an interesting conversation of her own, sounds like she's got a winner. …

Inside the office we listen in.

"Where am I? How did I get here?" a gentleman asks sounding a little groggy as he seems to be shaking the cobwebs out of his still spinning head.

"Don't you remember, you were telling me about this feeling, this desire? Go on." The woman's voice says going through her daily routine of questions as she shuffles her papers on her desk while pulling out a photo from a folder sitting the picture to the side.

"The feeling? Yes the feeling, this overwhelming desire. I don't know Doc it's like everyday I lose a little more control of myself. For instance I hit a guy yesterday for no reason at all, just walked up said hi and WHAM-O!" he says as a primal aggression begins to peek out from the depths of his soul.

"Did you scratch him?" she asks with concern in her voice while writing on a posted note and handing it off to a man in a dark suit she summoned with a nod. The patient notices the interaction recognizing it as odd before answering.

"I'm not sure... It all happened so fast. But you know what..." he says trying to impresses her but is interrupted by the Doc who shows him a picture of someone familiar.

"You won, surprise, surprise. Tell me have you had contact with this woman... say within the last week or so?" she asks already knowing the answer by the way he's staring at the picture Sammy just pulled out of the file.

"Yes for awhile now, wow she's really rocked my world." The man says as he sits back in his seat with a reminiscent grin while he fondly recollects his time with the mysterious woman in the photo.

"Do you have anyone who can account for your whereabouts last night besides your main squeeze? We picked her up just an hour before you?" the Doc asks as she motions for some rather large orderlies in canvas hazmat suits to join them just out of the patient's view.

"Well? No. Wait she's here, where is she? What have you done? Where are we? How do I know you're really a doctor?" the young man says as he tries to remember what he even did last night? It's all kind of hazy at the moment.

"I'm sorry to tell you but it's what you've done that got you here, you've been infected with a very rare disease. You're going to have to stay here... Just until we can treat you, of course, once you're cured you can be on your way." She says as the two oversized orderlies take hold with a deathly grip to escort the frustrated and confused man out and to his cage for processing.

Soon as it gets quiet Ollie knocks on the door. "Come in." she says and is instantly filled with joy and bewilderment to see her old friend, "Oliver Pendulum where in the world have you been, we were supposed to have lunch last week?"

"Hello Sammy, it's good to see you again. Looks like it's getting a little crazy around here, yeah sorry about that guess I lost track of time?" Ollie announces as he quietly shuts the door so that no one will barge in.

"You, Mr. Chronometer lose track of time, yeah right? What's her name?" Sammy says and is unprepared to say the least when Ollie answers.

"Sophia... Sophia Sinclair-Renault." Ollie quietly says as he pulls up a seat while he watches Sammy's face go from that of a joking expression to one of utter shock and surprise.

"No... Sophia Sinclair! Our Sophia Sinclair, the head of our organization Sophia Sinclair? The Sophia Sinclair that brought us out of the dark ages and into the age of technology, the same Sophia Sinclair that married the wealthy industrialist Conrad Renault! No you didn't she's like almost a hundred years old and bed ridden." Sammy says as she runs through all the reasons why he would be there. Ollie isn't a fan of the Jacks though he's never told Sammy why but he avoids them at all cost, so showing up now in the building proves it must be important.

"Yep that's the one, close she recently had her 91 birthday. But to tell the truth she's still quite spry for her age." Ollie adds while pulling out an old key and gently sliding it toward Sammy.

"I need you to please do me a solid and retrieve all the pages from whatever this key unlocks. Old buddy ole pal, pretty please with sugar on top." Ollie says with a smile as Sammy stares at a key she's only heard about in all her time with the bureau.

"How the HELL did you get that!?" Sammy says reaching for the key and hiding it knowing there's plenty of ambitious eyes and ears everywhere that will do anything to rise in the organization. It's a real cut throat workplace.

"It's a long story." Ollie says with a smile as he settles in knowing that only the whole story will suffice as payment for the favor.

"Well I've heard I got time to spare, so spill it." Sammy says as she sits back awaiting the tale that placed the legendary key to door 703 into her hands just as they are interrupted by someone urgently seeking entry to her office.

"Yes, what is IT!" Sammy yells and is rewarded with a crisis of catastrophic proportions.

"Mam! Subsection eight has a patient on the loose!" the inexperienced Jack announces on his first day of guard duty.

"Jacks we have a situation on level eight that requires your immediate attention." Sammy says with disgust at the incompetent new Jack who's more of the desk and paperwork type as appose to the furious soldiers she's been use too.

"What? Why are you still standing here? Go back to your post..." Sammy says as she sends out an order to secure all patients in their rooms.

"But?" he attempts to reason but is shut down instantly.

"NOW!" Sammy yells causing the new hire to freak out dropping his file dumping highly sensitive papers all over the floor before running out to join the hunt.

"You might as well get out of here Ollie I won't find a better opportunity to use this key. Swing by the house for dinner and I'll give you what I find after I get my story." Sammy says as she pulls out an oddly shaped handgun while discretely hiding the key on her persons.

"Oh and Ollie..." Sammy says as stops at the door before rushing away, "...Dinner is at 7 p.m."

Ollie smiles and with the twist of the dial he vanishes from time. He easily makes his way out of the chaotic place with out even being seen by the countless guards who look frozen in time as Ollie navigates the hallway of statues made possible by the chronometer. From the outside looking in it just looks like Ollie disappears from sight. ...

Ollie reappears outside the building on the sidewalk and leisurely begins his stroll to his favorite vintage speakeasy of the 1920's turned into a legitimate bar to wet his whistle happy to get out of that place when all of a sudden the sound of shattering glass followed by gun shots ring out in the air.

Tink-tink-t-tink, tink-tink, is the sound a small silver whistle makes as it bounces down the alley coming to a rest under Ollie's boot. Ollie looks down the alley and bam! Right in front of him stands a large feral beast clasping the frantic and incompetent Jack in her hands.

Slowly she creeps toward Ollie one claw digging into the building the other dragging the Jack as she gets ever closer. She snarls showing all her razor sharp teeth at Ollie who just grins at her while putting his finger to his lips in silence causing the she-wolf's ears to perk up in confusion.

Ollie slowly steps down with all his weight crushing the metal whistle flat on the pavement. The she-wolf's snarl disappears as she sniffs the air trying to catch Ollie's scent.

With little more than a wink Ollie continues on his way without alerting the Jacks to their escapee's current location. The she-wolf quickly snaps the neck of the Jack in her hand dropping him on the ground then darts across the road disappearing into the night. Her howl of freedom is heard for miles.

"It's going to be a long night for the Jacks. I definitely got time for a drink." Ollie says with a chuckle before disappearing as well. …

Chapter Two

Ancient History

"Ok, let's see it was during prohibition in the then mobster run era of the Windy City. The Chicago Outfit was all the rage for a lot of good reasons like running soup kitchens all the way up to providing college tuitions for those exceptional minds no matter where they found them. But they were also considered a scourge to society by the government officials for some of the worst crimes of the time as well.

My reason for being there was simple I worked... more like I assisted an old friend who I always felt sort of responsible for, since saving him as a child. He nicknamed me the Time Broker. I guess being the worlds only time manipulator had proven to be a valuable asset to my old friend." Ollie says as he watches Sammy's face fill with curiosity and the glow of the recently stoked fire in her study.

It's the perfect place for a story.

"Who was your friend?" Sammy asks and Ollie can't help but grin at her enthusiasm.

"Alfonse Gabriel Capone." Ollie simply says as the crowd of one goes wild including a loud pop and crackle from the fire!

"Bullshit! You knew Capone?!" Sammy blurts out with a look of jealous excitement.

"Yeah I inadvertently helped him join the Five Points Gang when I saved his life as a kid. I'm not sure why you're surprised? I've known the most famous and infamous characters of our time going back to the early 1900's." Ollie says before getting back to the story of the evening.

"You lie!" blurts out of Sammy's mouth before she can even stop it.

"Have I ever?" Ollie responds to his seemingly comatose listener.

"So how does Sophia tie in to this? Was Capone a wolf?" Sammy asks with a bit more confusion trying to figure it out.

"No he wasn't a wolf but unbeknownst to him, Capone had some wolves in his ranks. They were well hidden, completely loyal to there pack, and brutally violent in the way they followed their boss's orders giving Capone no concern to question what they were. Hell they were all monsters it's just that most of them weren't hiding claws and razor sharp teeth underneath their fancy suits.

But as hidden as they were they still drew the attention of you Jacks. The biggest problem your old co-workers had was that they weren't prepared for how dangerous, man is. Sure you all hunt werewolves for a living, but you do that with specialized tools that effect wolves. The men who ran with the pack were just as violent and unaffected by the whistle that stunned their friends, and that's how the first group of Jacks came up missing. All thanks to Machine Gun Jack.

So they changed tactics sending beauty to tame the beast and boy what a beauty she was, innocent and unsuspecting but with just a touch of eager curiosity. She posed as a rich heiress from over seas who was just here to take in the American life. Falling for her was as easy as breathing and she was aware the effect she had on men, using her talents to creep ever so close to her targets.

One by one the pack disappeared never suspecting a thing from the shy young girl just looking for a fun time. They never seemed to see her dark side till it was too late. I saw her for what she was from the get go. But she wasn't after my boy so I turned a blind eye.

I must admit I was curious to see what she would do, mostly out of boredom, being a long lived person such as myself, can cause everything to get a bit repetitive at times. Inadvertently we seemed to be drawn to one another like moths to a flame. Sophia convinced me to leave Chicago behind. We traveled the world..." Ollie pauses his story while gazing off lost in the thought of this still touchy memory.

"Ollie? You ok?" Sammy asks with a yawn drawing her old friend's attention back to the here and now. Truth is she was nearly lost to the land of dreams when Ollie stopped his story snapping her back to the here and now.

Ollie just gives a subtle grin before continuing as if nothing had happened knowing the soothing sound of his voice will lull her back to sleep momentarily.

"Sophia was my longest pause in this chaotic life I've lived. We walked in the park in the evenings, had lavish dinners at all the finest restaurants, watched the seasons change hand in hand, it was one of the only times I felt complete.

But with in all those good times a dark cloud was looming over me like a curse, it plagued me much like my father before me. Those who get too close to me fall victim to grizzly fate at hands of a monster.

And then one day it happened. I woke to find her missing, the house in shambles.

I searched the place over and found nothing except my journal lying on the floor under the upside down couch. I had just known my curse had caught up with me once more taking my love away. I've tried to stop him many times over the years in some of the most amazing and landscape changing fights the world has ever seen, though few have ever witnessed them. Never the less I've failed in every way. I don't know what I'm doing wrong.

I believed her murdered much like all the others in my incredibly long life slain by a deity, who only wants to see me dead.

It wasn't till months later I noticed many pages torn out of my journal in a section I wasn't too familiar with. I hadn't spent the time I should have to learn my father's work inside and out. So I had no idea what was actually gone.

I spent years traveling researching all of the sights my father had written about in the journal while learning the inner workings of the device he created. I kept myself shutoff from the world not willing to inflict my curse on anyone else.

That is until I met a young Jackie in a bit of a pinch and way over her head. I'm guessing it was a hazing mission gone wrong, wouldn't you say?" Ollie says with a little umpf on the end of it to catch his drowsy listener's attention back to the story before continuing with a smile. (Sammy was the young Jackie in trouble when she would've surely lost her life if not for a timely assist from the Time Broker himself.)

"I spent all this time wondering what happened to my pages until recently you mentioned her by her first name in one of your impromptu meetings with your Happy Jacks while I was present. I knew it had to be the same Sophia. I became obsessed with finding her and to be honest it didn't take long to find her thanks to the Jacks records room and...

...As fate would have it I reconnected with her on her 91st birthday, boy was she surprised. It's safe to say Sophia recognized me instantly as I did her.

"My, my Oliver time has been good to you hasn't it?" she said to me as she asked her nurse to wheel her to her bedroom escorting me along the way then excusing the nurse from the room leaving her alone with me. Something the nurse had been told never to do for any patient in Sophia's state, but she always liked Ms. Sophia. I guess I looked harmless enough to the nurse so reluctantly she obliged stepping out for a cup of coffee.

Soon as the door was closed Sophia pulls a small jewelry box out from its hiding spot. She gave me the key with a tear in her eye. She warned me that removing the contents would break the deal she made with her father many years ago. She had lived a long and adventurous life until she stole my pages, having gone into hiding soon after.

Sophia admitted her father pressured her into the marriage and pushed her into the shadows of obscurity within the battlefields of the Jacks. She said she'd always dreamed of me finding her.

We reconciled during the long conversation where she explained why she did it.

She swore she loved me and found out her father Sullivan Sinclair the then predominant head of the Jacks, wanted nothing more than my head on a stick and the Chronometer around his wrist. She traded the pages from my journal for my safety supposedly it was some kind of map that led to an amazing cavern of magic. That is if you can believe someone in her state of mind. ...

Don't worry it was a fair trade." Ollie says with a grin realizing Sammy is sound asleep and hasn't heard anything he just said.

"Did I turn her into a statue of fossilized stone? Or did I give her a thousand more generations to reflect on her crimes?" Ollie adds in a whisper with a shoulder shrug as if he didn't know the answer before adding "THE END!" causing Sammy to wake up.

Sammy gives a quick stretch having no idea what it was she last heard. Always enjoying Ollie's unique outlook on the history of the past Sammy walks over to the bookshelf fishing an envelope out from in between two books. It's weathered and torn a sign of its age.

"This wasn't easy to get, hope it helps." Sammy says with a smile still trying to take in all she's heard before adding, "By the way, you wouldn't do your ole buddy Sammy here a solid and check in on a freelancer for me. She's failed to make her last two check-ins'. It's on your way."

Ollie pulls out his lost pages to his dad's journal plus a note from Sophia. Ollie pockets the note for later then reunites his newly found pages with their home before getting up to stretch.

"Actually this is nowhere near where I'm headed." Ollie says as he ponders her request just to make her squirm.

"It would be if you took a plane or a bus or a car or anything besides a damn train." Sammy says with a little bit of vinegar in her tone. Sometimes she doesn't get Ollie's obsession with trains.

"Hey you know the rules. It's not that I don't trust automobiles it's the operators... too many drivers too many dangers." Ollie says before agreeing to look in on her missing Jack with a simple head nod.

"Thank you, so you really knew Capone?" is her final take on the whole story like that was the most unbelievable part. Ollie just smiles as he heads toward the door.

"Tell Nigel I'll see him next time." Ollie quietly says as he slips out of the house and into the night with a knew game plan on stopping the evil that's haunted him his entire life, after he does this favor for his friend of course. …

It's the following Friday,

Across the country a car pulls up in the driveway as the sun sets giving rise to the night.

Only a short drive from the Pacific, after a long day of running your usual daily errands that took up most of her time and nearly all of her money Brinly is just stepping into her bungalow apartment with some take out.

Obviously exhausted from her chores she drops her bags, kicks off her boots, and stretches out on her favorite piece of furniture, her couch.

She places the take out on the table beside an amazingly decorated photo album that seemingly matches the walls to a tee.

The walls from floor to ceiling in every room are decorated with paintings and pictures from Brinly's past revealing the loving atmosphere Brinly was raised in. Mixed in with all that joy are several news articles about various myths she's personally debunked with her published theories. It's more of a tribute to all the secrets of the world that are normally kept in the shadows.

Brinly runs her hand over her most epic unanswered question before she lifts the heavy album up to her lap. It seemed every story her Dad ever told her that wasn't about Jack had to do with the Chronometer, which is what Brinly calls the book. She spent a lifetime collecting all the pictures and stories inside that describe the chronometer in detail with added notes Brinly has scribbled into the corners for reference.

Upon opening the album the first page is dedicated to the Unvanished. Brinly thumbs through the book taking time to study her favorite stories before turning her attention to the file the professor gave her.

Hours later, amidst a pile of greasy wrappers and empty containers Brinly gives a long stretch and a yawn. She slides the heavy book off her lap noticing the red mark it left behind in its absence with a grin.

"Let's go Brin, you got a big day tomorrow." Brinly tells herself before turning off the lights and making her way to the bedroom. …

Beep-Beep-Beep-Beep-Beep-Beep-Beep-Beep-Beep-Beep-Beep-Beep-Beep-Beep-Beep-Beep-Beep-Beep-Beep-Beep-Beep-Beep-Beep-Beep-Beep-Beep-Beep

The alarm clock finally does its job after only forty five minutes of ear-splittingly annoying chirps as Brinly starts to show signs of life.

Another late night another crazy dream, she'd be the first to admit she's always had an active imagination but some of her dreams are on another level of 'what the hell'.

She recognizes the improbability of it all as always while leaving a sliver of hope that it was real. Brinly's always in trouble in her dreams but able to escape thanks to a monster that shows up out of nowhere scaring whoever is chasing her away. It's a nice dream but that's all, just a dream.

Brinly stretches for a moment before getting up and making her way into the bathroom. Normally she'd just turn the alarm off and go back to sleep. But today is a day she's been waiting on for what feels like forever.

It's finally here the Saturday of the Followers of the Guise gathering.

The goal is to head out as soon as possible having already packed up her car for the trip. Brinly plans on finding 5020 Cypress Lane by lunch time set up a camp in the woods just out of sight of the gathering place where she'll hide her car with the best escape route in case things get hairy. Then snoop around a bit before the party to see what she can uncover about the Followers.

Brinly always loved camping. She went a lot as a child with her Mom and Dad creating the fondness that fueled her many camping trips ever since.

So twenty minutes later she's out on the open road coffee in hand with adventure in her sights and a map to where to find it. …

Off the beaten path in the small town of Paradise, California, home of the infamous Cypress Lane, the train slowly comes to a stop in a cloud of steam and smoke. These tracks use to carry the life blood of the country across its tracks. Thousands upon thousands of people found their freedom right here where these tracks ended. But with time like all things the railroad was pushed to the side by progress reduced to the carriers of the mail while the automobile took over the entire known world.

Ollie never trusted the these new forms of travel, he may look young but he's seen more in his ninety plus years than most of the rest of us could ever dream of. The dangerous early years of the automobile and their drivers was enough to keep him off the road.

The door on one of the box cars slides open revealing the outside world to Ollie who waves at the postman who allowed him to hitch a ride as he hops out and disappears within the clouds at the station.

Ollie hasn't any time to waste he's waited so long to get his missing pages back that all he wants to do is head to the coordinates described in his father's notes. If he's reading this right his next stop after finding Sammy's freelancer is Las Vegas, well the dessert outside of the booming city of lights at least.

It's been over twenty years since Ollie roamed around the town with no locks and no clocks, where anyone could be rich in the roll of the dice. Ollie smiles as he reflects on the infamous card game that still fills his memory.

It was in the fifties when Benny Binion hosted a poker game that lasted months. Ollie just happened to bump into one of the players, Johnny Moss on a day like any other as they both we're headed to the casino from the hotel.

Mr. Moss was like a magician with the cards he just seemed to have it all figured out. But even with all that talent the one thing he lacked was time. Nobody knew Johnny was fighting a battle all by himself an internal struggle to survive, maybe that's what made the game come easy for him though he never looked happy as he played.

"If only I had a little more time?" Moss said under his breath while the elevator slowly crept to the gaming floor. Moss didn't even notice Ollie in elevator with him. "How much would you need?" Ollie asked surprising the quiet and usually conservative Moss.

"Jesus boy! You could've given me a heart attack." Moss says with a slight grin.

"Oh I'm sure you would've bluffed your way out of it, knowing you." Ollie chuckles and again asks, "How much would you like, a year, two, or twenty? What's your pleasure?"

"If you're really asking that can mean only one thing, you know the Time Broker?" Moss says with a smile causing Ollie to grin from ear to ear.

"I haven't been called that in a very long time." Ollie responds while revealing the Chronometer on his wrist. Ollie turns the dial once then twice before hitting the button giving Mr. Moss a new lease on life.

"Twenty it is. Now that's not enough to change your looks too drastically, though everyone will swear you look like a younger man. Just smile and enjoy. Never tell them where you got it." Ollie said and watched as Johnny walked away with a bit more spring in his step.

The rest as they say is history. I believe Johnny took his opponent Nick the Greek for two million dollars during the marathon game breaking the player in the process and inspiring what the world come to know as the World Series of Poker.

But it was the grace at which the two players had that earned Ollie's respect. Moss never bragged or put his opponent down during or after the match and at the end Nick the Greek simply said,

"I'm sorry Mr. Moss but I'm going to have to let you go."

Now it's one thing to win with grace, but to lose, to lose with the same grace is a skill Ollie has yet to pick up.

Needless to say just thinking about all his old times has gotten Ollie excited about his next stop, but first things first, find the freelancer.

Then VEGAS! …

Chapter Three

Secrets & Societies

It's dusk outside a yet to be open gated community complete with thirty six hole golf course and a crystal clear lake called Cypress Estates. Down the freshly paved lane at the end of the recently poured concrete still in its curing process sits a magnificent representation of what it means to live the good life just begging to be occupied. It's the first house to get a for sale sign in the yard.

5020 Cypress Lane, Paradise, California, is the gravel driveway sitting beside the opulent new house ready to be sold.

The driveway takes you back into the woods away from the community away from the light leading you into a large nature preserve on one side of the lake allowing abundant wildlife to roam the grounds to add to the obeisance of the 'Getting Away From It All' feel the place has. This is where the party will be.

When Cypress Estates opens it's sure to cater to the wealthy. But tonight it's reserved for those loyal to the Guise whose connections grow far and wide. And by the looks of it there's already movement in the woods near the large stone mansion built more like a castle than a home. The extensive use of rocks blends in well with the large trees that engulf it.

Upstairs Brinly has roamed all around the lavishly decorated house before the gathering finding absolutely nothing to back up any of her theories about the Followers. She's at the point of calling it quits and getting out of there before she's found snooping when she hears a noise coming from down the hall.

Turning opposite the noise she rushes away taking the next left without even looking resulting in her running into another snooping person looking for her.

"Whoa excuse me I'm sorry, I'm not sure I'm in the right place?" Ollie sheepishly says having watched Brinly go into the house from the tree line choosing to follower her in when he saw the car pull up.

But before Brinly has a chance to respond a flashlight is aimed at her face in an interrogation style while a voice shouts out asking why they're here?

The Chronometer catches Brinly's eye instantly as its wearer reaches for it looking to make his escape. Brinly lightly brushes his hand stopping him in his tracks as she turns to respond.

"WE dreamed of the address, we were called here." Brinly says causing the security detail to chuckle.

"Yeah we always get a few early birds around here." he says while pointing toward a set of double doors and the only ones Brinly couldn't open when she was snooping around.

"Make yourself at home we'll be starting in just a bit." The man says as he turns off his flashlight while escorting the two new recruits through the double doors.

Brinly can't help but be in awe as all is revealed upon walking through the now opened double doors. Floor to ceiling tapestries depicting the long history of the Guise are hung from the rafters. There's paintings and poems hanging on the walls and on the second floor of the large room there's a library filled with hand written accounts and stories about the Followers and their benevolent god, the Guise.

Brinly holds the Chronometer's hand tight as she pulls him along while keeping her eyes on all the tapestries reading each and every word and taking in every detail painstakingly sewn into them.

"They're very nice." Ollie says referring to the tapestries with a smile before adding, "Listen if you're going to continue to hold on to me we should at least have a proper introduction. Don't you think?"

"Promise you won't up and vanish on me?" Brinly asks with a smile letting on that she knows more about Ollie than even he realizes.

"I'm not the vanishing type." is Ollie's subtle response causing Brinly to snicker.

"Hi, I'm Brinly but my friends call me Brin." She says with a smile so contagious it catches Ollie off guard causing a similar reaction out of him.

"I'm Ollie." He mutters as she drags him up to the second floor still on the hunt for answers.

"So what brings you all the way out here in the middle of nowhere?" Brin asks as she picks up a small book that kind of reminds her of her own book about the Chronometer. "Mine's bigger." She thinks to herself.

"You." Ollie coyly says drawing Brinly's full attention back to the here and now as she sits the small book down while keeping her hand firmly on it as if it might try and escape.

"You missed a few check-in's with your employer. They got concerned. You don't know what they are, do you?" Ollie says as he wanders around taking no interest in this world of the Guise.

"Yes, they're an ends to a means for me and that's all. So they sent you? Lucky me." Brin says, saying more of what was on her mind than she wanted.

Their attraction is obvious.

"Funny, I thought I was the lucky one." Ollie chuckles as he steps over and whispers, "You want to know about the Guise? I can tell you things about the Guise that'd curl your toes and turn you white as a ghost. More than what's in these books."

Just then before Brin could even respond to Ollie's comment the doors swing open as a large group of people flood into the sacred space. Brinly quickly pockets the small book when Ollie wasn't looking for research purposes of course.

Ollie and Brin make their way downstairs consciously keeping to the back of the crowd and wow there's a lot of them. They're all chanting in different languages causing the place to fill with incoherent noise until the lights dim.

A sweet yet overpowering voice takes center stage and as soon as his followers hear it the room goes silent.

"It is I!" the voice calls out to his people.

"AND I AM IT." the crowd responds in unison.

"We are one." Again the voice calls out to his crowd.

"BECAUSE OF HIM." the crowd retorts again with even more volume than the last.

"Brothers and Sisters, the true Followers of the Guise I welcome you. I am their leader Unger Reese. Pledge your loyalty to the Guise and never feel unloved again." the voice now given the name Unger Reese replies as he guides the group outside on the grounds of this gem hidden away from the world.

Brinly's floored by what she sees out on the lawn having figured maybe a sacrificial alter and throne of skulls from the way Unger's appearance and demeanor played out to the crowd.

Brinly is surprised that nothing could be further from the truth as the glow from hundreds of twinkling lights gives off the warm and inviting feeling that grows from all the tables set up with fine delicacies.

That's when Ollie sees him just off in the distance of the forest. He catches Ollie's eye in an instant and suddenly the reason to stay has diminished completely.

"You need to get out of here, RIGHT NOW." Ollie says as he now won't let go of Brinly's hand.

"What are you talking about? Why would we leave? Look I'm here to learn whatever I can about the Guise. I've got a job to do." Brinly says as something shiny in the forest catches her eye.

"Listen you're fixing to get an up close and personal look at the Guise himself, you'll be lucky to survive it." Ollie says as he pulls her inside just as the deity appears in the middle of his mesmerized followers as Unger reaches out to him.

"I'm telling you this is fixing to get bad so stay out of sight. Those people whoever they are, are the sacrifices, he's going to kill them all if I don't stop him. He's here for only one thing... to haunt me." Ollie says realizing this has been one of Corvan's more elaborate traps.

"My children, how long has it been? Look at you all prospering out in the world I gave to you. Belly's full, out of the elements, nothing to challenge your rule over the planet." The deity says in such a heavenly tone that all who hears it instantly swoon. Though that could be all in thanks to the body he possessed being that of Unger Reese himself.

"There is one among us my children that doesn't belong. Where is he?" the deity asks as the entranced group slowly turns like zombies to point out the new recruits finding no one there.

"Where are you Oliver? No reason to hide from me now, I know you're here." the deity says.

Ollie turns to look at Brinly for only a moment before saying, "Get the people inside the castle as fast as you can. The thick stone walls will protect you all. Stay away from the windows."

Suddenly Ollie disappears in front of Brinly's eyes instantly reappearing out in the courtyard where the followers and their god are.

"I thought I smelt a Pendulum." The deity says as Ollie steps through the crowd with his only thoughts of getting his hands around the throat of the deity in whatever form he takes.

"Murderer." Ollie says with his blood instantly boiling as it always does when he gets his chance to avenge his parent's deaths. Ollie's had many chances over the years each battle ending the same way, with Ollie leaving the deity trapped inside its own petrified body.

The crowd parts, giving plenty of distance to the chronometer as he slowly makes his way up to where a wild eyed and floating Unger resides.

"Child you can't blame me for your father's poor choices. He could've given me the Chronometer centuries ago and spared all those countless families he sired but still he chose to let you all die instead. I think if anything I would be blaming your dear ole daddy for your current predicament." The Guise says through the evil grin of the possessed man the deity currently dwells in.

The toxic comment hits its mark as Ollie balls up his fist and launches a feverous attack ending with Ollie hitting the Chronometer taking the possessed Unger Reese and himself out of the danger of the crowd in the courtyard and putting the fight in a more secluded place off in the woods.

Ollie quickly twists the many dials like a combination lock before hitting the Chronometer again. A dome of blue light shoots from his wrist encapsulating Unger's possessed body.

There's a slight breeze in the night time air that gains Ollie's attention as it sweeps over the back of his right ear as soft and subtle as a lover's kiss goodbye. Ollie takes a second enjoying the breeze before responding.

"You're going to look at me one way or another Corvan." Ollie rattles off as he watches as Unger's body begins aging at a remarkable rate until it becomes a shriveled corpse turning to dust soon after.

Left in the cult leaders place inside the time bubble from hell is a light blue faceless form. It hovers just above the ground in a somewhat proud stance at defying gravity. The form turns to Ollie and it's obvious that it can see even without eyes.

"You think you've saved them, they were never yours to save. Therefore you never could've, she's in there now." Corvan says unfazed by the time being taken from him.

"Who's she?" Ollie asks as he turns to listen in the distance of the night only hearing an eerie silence.

"My child my flesh and blood, she's hunting them down as we speak sparing none except for those who wear her mark." Corvan gloats as the screams break the tree line coming from the house.

"Do you know how many wear the mark?" Corvan asks in a jovial way as Ollie twists the dials once more before stopping to look at this monster that plagues him.

With a breath of disgust Ollie spoils the deity's fun, "None."

Ollie hits the Chronometer sending a surge of energy out dropping the gloating god to the ground turning his light out in the process. Ollie walks over to the lifeless mannequin, postures for only a second before kicking him straight in the face, a parting gift as Ollie rushes to save Brinly. …

Back at the large stone mansion it's in a wash of blood. No body escaped whatever this was. Ollie quietly walks around the place going room to room searching for Brinly when a noise catches his attention from up stairs. It's a crunching sound followed by a low growl. A paw print on the floor clues him in that the low growl is accompanied by some large feet.

Ollie slips through time making his way up to the source behind the door at the end of the hall. But before Ollie can get the drop on it, all goes quiet inside. He realizes that whatever it is, it senses when danger is close.

Kicking in the door Ollie finds only bodies, several bodies piled up in the center of the room with each one missing limbs. Ollie investigates and finds that all evidence points to an animal attack by the way the bodies are chewed up. But something just doesn't feel right and that's when he hears it.

That same low growl so strong that it causes the floor to vibrate from its tone, Ollie turns to find nothing then suddenly feeling the hot breath of a beast, breathing down his neck. Slowly he twists the dials before pressing play, sending a jolt through the castle and causing the unwanted guest to make her very first appearance.

At a loss for words for what he sees as a enormous tiger the size of a van adorning a set of rams horns and a king cobra with a mind connected to it's own for a tail materializes right in front of him.

It's obvious the blast pissed it off, but aside from that Ollie thinks this may be more difficult than he thought. That jolt was ten thousand years and it didn't even phase it.

Without moving so much as a muscle the Chimera showing its blood drenched teeth creeps slowly closer until her nose is only inches away from Ollie's face. Ollie can feel tiny droplets of blood hitting his cheek as the beast exhales on him.

Time seems to stand still as he ever so slightly eases his hand over to his wrist. The Chimera opens her mouth laying her tongue on Ollie's face like an ever so loving pet.

Ollie starts to hit her with a double dose of what he zapped Corvan with it the woods, about three hundred thousand years. When Ollie suddenly stops realizing for whatever reason the beast has no interest in eating him.

The beast slowly circles him with a low growl before it busts through wall after wall till it launches itself outside vanishing in the process.

Ollie rushes down the stairs but stops to find Brinly covered in blood and nothing else just outside the front door. She looks out of sorts until she sees Ollie.

"Oh my God Ollie something was in here, something was after them. I'm sorry I must've passed out, but I heard when it arrived.

I was really close to it, I think?" Brinly says as she reaches out to Ollie before dropping to the ground.

Ollie is confused but happy to see her as he helps her back to her feet. "Yeah it nearly got me too, come on we got to get out of here." Ollie says as they step out of the safety the followers' headquarters afraid of what's waiting for them in the woods.

"Our best route of escape would be that way." Brin says as she points toward the tree line to the west end of the house which is dangerously close to where Ollie left Corvan who by all accounts should be waking up any moment now.

Ollie glances behind the house as they run noticing the bodies covering the lawn like a blanket. There's so much blood running down the slightly sloping lawn that it looks like a raging river.

Ollie pulls Brinly close so as to not allow her to see anymore carnage left in the wake of Corvan's beast. "We got to get you out of here!" Ollie says fearing he's condemned Brinly's life simply by standing by her for Corvan to see.

"He's killed everyone I've ever loved." Ollie quietly states as they break through the tree line. The wind eerily whispers to *'Run for your life…'*

"Are you saying you love me?" Brinly says while perking up to see which way she set up camp which at the moment is beyond difficult.

"Of course not, we've just met. But Corvan doesn't know that and if I'm being totally honest I doubt he cares. You've been spotted with me and that's all it takes, for that… I'm sorry" Ollie says while noticing the forest come to terrifying life right in front of their eyes.

The trees of the forest begin to reach out at them the branches scratch and rake at Brinly's face and hair while attempting to peel the Chronometer off Ollie's wrist.

Brinly shuts her eyes clinching onto Ollie's arm after not being able to find his hand when suddenly all is quiet. Brinly opens her eyes to find the nightmare from Oz over as she's standing in the center of what looks an energy shield of some sorts keeping all but the two of them out.

"You are the Unvanished! I knew it." Brinly says without even looking at Ollie. She's so enamored by the bubble of time that encases them allowing nothing to penetrate the shield. Brinly slowly wanders over to the edge getting dangerously close to the barrier.

"That's not a good idea." Ollie quickly warns Brinly as her hand reaches out attempting to touch the curiously crackling wall of energy with her index finger.

Brinly instantly halts without removing her hand from its most perilous situation while simply looking back for a better explanation.

"That's ten million years of time you see before you. It loops back and fourth and back and fourth from the ground to the peak creating this force field of time. Anything that touches it including monstrous trees controlled by a deity will have that same amount of time pulled from them. So please unless you're an immortal don't touch it." Ollie says as he softly reaches over her shoulder pulling her arm down and away from the dome of time.

She's fascinated, Brinly puts her ear just a little closer without touching the shield. She listens to the sizzle and popping of time in its rawest form as it's harnessed by a man as easy as riding a bike.

Snapping his fingers to get Brinly out of her mesmerizing trance Ollie reminds her of the still impending danger all around them saying, “We should probably be leaving now.”

So rushing into the camp sight Ollie stops in his tracks as he sees her means of escape, “That’s your idea of an escape route?”

“Well it’s not a train but under our current circumstances it’ll have to do.” Brinly says as she wipes her self off before throwing on her spare change of clothes and hoping in her car.

With little options and feeling a need to keep Brinly safe Ollie simply says, “A leap of faith.” before hopping in the passenger side just as Brinly races away…

Chapter Four

Yankee Doodle comes to Town

Ring-ring, ring-ring, ring-ring, ring-ring, ring-ring, ring-ring, ring-ring, ring-ring, ring-ring, ring-ring, ring-ring, ring-ring, ring-ring…

It's the middle of the day in a rundown record shop called Yankee Doodle's. The phone has been ringing off the wall for the last ten minutes. Finally the door that leads to the mysterious basement bursts open with a tall rather lanky man with a large Mohawk dressed in spikes and leather emerging from the depths while wiping his hands. The towel he is using use to be a pastel yellow but now it's a blood soaked red.

The lanky man shouts and points as if to keep quiet to whatever was down there with him before slamming the door and rushing to answer the phone.

"Yankee Doodles, if we ain't got it you don't want it. How can I help you?" the lanky man says and is thrown off guard at what he is told.

"Suit up Jack your dream gig has got the green light. The Time Broker's card has been pulled, he's up for retirement.

You're going to have to hustle to beat the other agent to the punch. The Broker is headed south on State Route 395, if I've figured correctly you can catch him around Bishop. Good luck." The voice on the other end of the line says before hanging up.

The lanky punk rocker just stands there mesmerized by his good fortune. It's been decades since anyone has gone after the Broker with the Jacks consent and even then the consent didn't come from the top.

Twenty years ago there was a cue within the Jacks organization known as 'The War of the Twelves'. The twelfth generation of Jacks was tired of following the path laid out for them by their predecessors. So they set out to snatch the Broker up before anyone would even know while blazing a new path for themselves.

It was an off the books operation with the consequence for their actions being death in the harshest of ways set to match each conspirators behavior.

Yankee's uncle on his mother's side was a causality of The War of the Twelves' but not by the punishment. Uncle Jack was killed during the raid to take the Chronometer at the hands of non-other than the Broker himself.

Uncle Jack was a good man Yankee remembers, as he locks the front door turning his open sign to 'sorry we're closed' while reminiscing about the good old days.

... He was a youngster only about eight when it had happened, his uncle Jack had come for a visit that summer and Yankee's dad wanted no part of it, saying that his wife's brother was a deadbeat who wouldn't amount to nothing. They lived in upstate New York at the time and all was right with the world. But over that summer a lot of unexplainable disappearances started happening. It wasn't long before their little town began pointing fingers at Yankee's family more specifically his Uncle as the reason for the disappearances.

Yankee's Uncle Jack would spend hours telling his nephew stories about a secret group he had heard about while playing with Yankee's toy soldiers. All the adventures the secret group would go on and the monsters they hunted to make the world a safer place. He always recognized the keen mind his nephew had as he watched the young Yankee clear the board using his strategy.

"You know I'm one of them too. And when you're ready there will be a spot waiting for you in their ranks." Uncle Jack told Yankee on his last night in town. The call Uncle Jack was waiting on had finally come in with a new set of directives. Uncle Jack had to slip away in the night never to be seen again.

It was never clear to Yankee what his Uncle had done to have to leave in such a secret way. He just always saw him as his fun loving Uncle. If only he knew that would've been the last time he would see him. Yankee would've stopped him from going, begged him to stay…

If only…

Yankee's Dad came to school a few days later to pick up his son instead of the mom who usually did those types of things. Upon getting in the car Yankee was surprised and unhappy to see his Dad, his dad never seemed to care for him like his Mom or even his Uncle. All his Dad ever did was to complain about life.

There was sorrow in his father's eyes as Yankee closed the door. "Your Uncle is gone your mother hasn't taken the news very well. Also we're moving away for a job offer I couldn't refuse. We leave in the morning." Yankee's Dad tells him as they pull off from the school never to return. …

It was only two years later when Yankee's Mom chose another path leaving her husband a widow and her son lost to the world. Yankee grew up feeling more and more abandoned and bitter while his father never seemed to care.

As a teenager Yankee thrived in the underground music scene living a Punk Rock lifestyle finding his refuge in the Big Apple of all places until one day the Jacks came a calling.

Yankee jumped at the chance to escape his ulcer of a father to be like his Uncle and the Jacks had a role that needed to be filled quickly. Observe and report was the task given to Yankee and he made it look as effortless as breathing it was safe to say that Yankee was born to be a Jack.

Yankee wound up taking a wolf out completely single handed while capturing its mate. He lead the two wolf pack into a jewelry store incapacitating the female and wrapping her up in silver chains while shoving a hand full of silver down the male's throat then forcing it to swallow, the indigestion was too much for the wolf.

Yankee's reward earned his spot on the Jacks roster. Boy was he good, Yankee shot up the ranks in a legendary pace. There wasn't a challenge he couldn't tackle no task he ever left incomplete. It's safe to say Yankee possessed all the traits and skills necessary to one day lead the organization. But that would never be the case you see Yankee had a tendency to stick his nose into the case that haunted him his whole life, the death of his Uncle, The War of the Twelves, and The Time Broker.

Still Yankee managed to reach the top ten list of highest number of retirees before getting demoted to interrogation and disposal duty at a safe house out in the middle of nowhere California for simply not dropping it.

Yankee has gotten close to catching the Broker over the last few years but never able to break the truce long enough to nab him. Now all of a sudden they've lifted the protection on the Time Broker and Yankee had to hear it from an old buddy still working inside the Chicago office.

Yankee walks down the stairs to end his interrogation session before torching the evidence in the disposal room. Then he heads to his quarters in the underground bunker attached to the basement. The excitement fills every fiber of his being as Yankee opens an old trunk in his closet revealing his old battle suit meant to be worn under your natural clothing. It was made out of a material Yankee could never identify but only the elite Jacks had the suits.

Giving you a clue at just how good Yankee really is.

The suit was a safety net for its wearer thanks to the fact it was bullet proof, impervious to fire, and enhanced the wearer's strength for brief periods of time. Though out of all of its remarkable features was its ability to momentarily shield it's wearer from the chronometer's touch. This was the most useful power to its wearer when trying to escape.

Yankee slips into the suit that was made for him before adorning his signature leather vest and pants totally bedazzled with spikes while glancing in the mirror to make sure his hair is on point.

Yankee grabs a nap sack filled with an assortment of the Jacks greatest weapons and a stack of eight tracks. Yankee hops in his ride with a map in his hands and his sights set on Bishop, California in search of his day to bask in the glorious sun of revenge.

Yankee tingles with hope of tearing the Chronometer off the Broker's wrist and taking every second of life he's got stored inside him as he fires up his chopped lead sled.

Popping in his favorite eight track by the Clash he lights a cigar while punching the gas rocketing off toward his destiny…

On the opposite end of a long journey.

Out on the open road nearing the town of Bishop Brinly asks the burning question she's been dying to ask ever since she realized who Ollie really was.

"So tell me how you came to be standing on that platform all by yourself so many moons ago?" Brinly asks as she looks at Ollie with a look on her face like the answer will set her free.

"I've read the Unvanished but I want your side of the story." She adds with a slight smile as she continues to head south.

"I wasn't by myself that night...

The train left only slightly behind schedule as me and my newly reunited father take the time to rest a bit after escaping certain death. The wait for the train was some of the most terrifying moments of my life. Not knowing if the monster from my house would find us before we boarded the train, we were headed west was all I knew at the moment.

Once we boarded and were shown to our cabin on the train I relaxed but only slightly. It wasn't till the train was in motion and we had locked our cabin's door that I finally felt safer. He looked at me and smiled, "You look like your mother Oliver."

Dad showed me his journal and explained how he created the Chronometer out of a mysterious material he found out in the desert over two hundred and fifty years ago.

“I’m going to show you how to use this watch to your advantage though I feel I’ve only scratched the surface on what it may be capable of. I’ve taken many notes over the years on what I’ve discovered beyond what I designed it for and kept them all in this journal. The answer on how to stop the Guise is here.”

Then he admitted to me how old he was which, was something my mother always wondered, you ready, he was three hundred and nine years old. I was too young to really even understand, my only question was where has he been?

“My boy I’ve been all over the world a hundred times over, in this book I’ve mapped out where I’ve hid collections of treasures so massive we’ll only have to worry about one thing.”

“The Monster?” I replied softly.

Then he told me about the one thing, his curse a true scourge to humanity, a vindictive deity who wanted the Chronometer for himself. The deity’s name was Corvan Sin or as those idiots back there like to call him...The Guise.

Corvan Sin ‘the Guise’ is the closest thing to a God you will ever see.

It was the Guise that murdered my mother. Corvan haunted my father for centuries killing everyone my father loved. You see the Guise couldn’t hurt my father while he wore the Chronometer but he could take away the ones closest to my father. My father was working on a way to permanently stop the Guise when he caught wind that Corvan had discovered my existence. My father couldn’t bear to lose me too.

So as we disembarked in Sacramento our planned destination I felt a slight chill in the air that night on the platform. Dad stopped to take the time to put his coat around me he tucked his journal away in the coat's pocket. Dad also placed the Chronometer around my wrist. It was like he sensed Corvan's presence or something. He whispered something to me as we stood there. He told me to find the Erased.

I didn't even know what he was talking about as I watched his expression go from that of a caring Father to that of angry monster.

There was people walking all around us but all I saw at the end of the platform was the silhouette of a man who laughed at my dad's attempt to escape him.

We slowly make our way through the crowd toward the stairs as my father stopped and took a moment to just be, I guess he was tired of running. It's like time stood still as my dad looked at me with a smile on his face. He chuckles about some of the fun we had on the train and then he announced out loud.

"You're in range."

"Ha ha-ha-hahaha, please Barty boy I'm no fool. I know you won't kill your son let alone all these people just to postpone the inevitable." the silhouette says with a chuckle taunting us as he slowly creeps closer. Those that overhear his words begin to flee while others pay the monster no mind.

My father grins ear to ear causing the man to take pause as my father turns ever so subtly revealing the Chronometer resting on my wrist before responding, "You're right."

"NO DON'T!!" Corvan shouts but it was too late my father had set the dials and hit the button. He scarified himself and everybody else on that platform just so I wouldn't die.

In a flash that looked like an exploding star everybody was gone... he was gone. The train was aged a million years in the blink of an eye utterly destroying it along with the whole station and several cars back. The wood beneath my feet had turned to stone all the people around us vanished leaving me alone.

I had absorbed all the time my Dad had set the Chronometer to take from the area. And it now coursed through my body like the fountain of youth itself. ...

"Why not just go back in time and save him?" Brinly asks with a genuine curiosity knowing very little about the actual Chronometer. Everything she's learned was just story passed down from one person to the next, much like the theory that the Chronometer is a time travel device.

Brinly notices her odometer click a couple more miles on it before Ollie decides to answer having been just staring off into the night.

"If only, if only this were a device to travel through time. Oh what a world it would be. You know I've hoped on more than one occasion that it could do exactly that." Ollie snickers at his response knowing he's nearly driven himself insane over the thought throughout his many years.

"Sadly it doesn't work like that. I can do many things with this wonderful time piece.

I can manipulate time on a whim, slow it down till a rushing river is as still as a painting hung in a museum.

I can take the time from anything in my designated area until there's nothing left and freely give to whom ever I want.

But...no matter how many times I've tried, no matter how many times I've still yet to try. I can't reverse the flow of time it's too vast to control, it would be like a pebble holding back the flow of the ocean.

Instead the immense ocean of time crashes all around me while I stay untouched by it with the Chronometer on my wrist. And as long as I wear this time piece the deity I know as Corvan Sin can't get me.

Thing is he's immortal and all I've ever been able to do is slow him down same as my Dad. I turned him into a statue once that lasted a month before he got free. And since I only need a second to disappear from the eyes of the world. I could always make my escape." Ollie says as he hears a clicking noise causing him to take his head off the window to see where they are.

"When you think there's nothing else around you, you'll find a Breakfast House. I bet there's a Breakfast House on the moon." Brinly says with a chuckle about the restaurant chain that seems to have it's diners in the most remote of places.

She pulls off the road and into one of many empty parking spots at the Breakfast House before looking at Ollie and asking, "Then why fight him?"

"Corvan killed my family. How could I not? I won't truly be free till I stop him forever. I just don't know how to do it, yet. All in good time though as they always say. I know the answers are in this book." Ollie responds as he seems more excited than usual to hop out and stretch his legs. Brinly pauses for only a second thinking about his answer 'How could he not' as if he's accepted the fact that he'll never get his revenge and at the same time he'll never stop trying.

'That is a curse.' Brinly thinks to herself.

"You know they have the best milkshakes." Ollie adds with a smile as Brinly points out an old lead sled parked at the far end of the lot. "Nice, it looks like a '49 Merc." Ollie says as he follows her in the front door. ...

In the driver's seat of the lead sled at the far end of the lot Yankee sits waiting for just the right moment to make his move. Disgruntled or not Yankee follows the Jacks code without resolve. The most important of all their rules is to not harm the innocent.

'KNOWING WHAT WE KNOW DOESN'T CHANGE WHAT WE HAVE TO DO.' – Words of Jack wisdom.

So with a puff of his cigar Yankee changes out the eight track and continues to wait for the moment to strike watching as another car pulls into the lot, Yankee recognizes the driver.

"Well this just got interesting."...

Years ago, when Yankee was green in the ways of the Jacks he had to deal with Barley. His real name was Wilson Barley but everyone just called him Barley. He was a generation or two older than Yankee having worked alongside Yankee's Uncle Jack. Barley had a fierce reputation and a retiree count that looked to be reaching epic. Though rumor has it that not all of Barley's kills were of lupine origin. Barley was an asshole of the highest order in Yankee's truest opinion.

Barley hated Yankee for lots of reasons like his stature, his charm, and how he made the job look easy. From Yankee's trial by fire to get in the Jacks organization to the record number of retirees' Yankee racked up his first year as a Jack. There was no denying one day Yankee would pass Barley's record no matter what Barley did. And out of all these reasons there was none more prevalent than the fact that Yankee is the nephew to Barley's old partner and it made his blood boil.

Seeing Yankee's car at the end of the near empty lot prompts Barley's actions as he slams his car into park in the spot beside Yankee. Barley rolls down his window and motions Yankee to do the same, excited at the ass chewing he's fixing to give. Sadly for Barley, Yankee's response was to simply give him the bird from behind his still rolled up glass. …

Inside the deserted looking Breakfast House sitting at their choice of empty booths Ollie and Brin look over the menu. Suddenly in a burst of commotion the waitress/cook comes out of the back looking like she's been asleep for the better part of the night.

"It's a good morning for breakfast, what'll you have?" the waitress announces the Breakfast House's mandatory greeting with a salty spin on the end.

"I'll have the Philly Cheese Steak melt and shredded potatoes, sizzled, blanketed, sliced, and porcupined." Brinly rattles off as she isn't even sitting due to the fact she's about to pee her pants.

"Porcupined?" Ollie announces loudly at Brin who's rushing to the ladies room, recognizing all the other ways to get your potatoes he just curious what it could stand for.

“It’s chopped jalapeños!” Brin shouts back before disappearing behind the swinging door by the jukebox.

“Make it two, plus a couple of colas, thank you mam, sorry for showing up at this time of night.” Ollie says with a wink causing the tired waitress to smile.

“Oh no worries darling, I needed to stretch my legs anyways. So what brings you out here in the middle of nowhere?” the waitress asks as she cracks three eggs over the hot grill, the sizzling sound is quickly followed by the wonderful smell of breakfast that fills the air.

Ollie just raises an eyebrow to her actions, neither he nor Brinly ordered eggs yet its eggs the waitress is cooking. But at this time of night food is food, be it a Philly cheese steak melt or good old fashioned breakfast. So Ollie leaves the waitress to her work as he waits for his company.

It isn’t long before the correct order is delivered piping hot on two plates while Brinly has yet to return. Suddenly the bell rings indicating more customers have just walked in. Recognizing the trouble the old lady’s in Ollie keeps it simple, “Would you be so kind to check on my date for me I’m starting to worry.”

“No problem Sugar.” she says with a wink after taking a bite of the fried eggs she made for herself while she was cooking, she doesn’t even look back while adding, “Take a seat I’ll be right with ya.”

Ollie watches the look of the tall lanky man who seems obviously put off by his acquaintance that seemed to be fighting to walk in first stands there looking overly angry.

The lanky man throws an elbow out of nowhere knocking his angry little cohort out before making his way toward Ollie.

'SOMETIMES YOU HAVE TO DO WHAT'S BEST, NOT WHAT'S RIGHT. SOMETIMES WHAT'S BEST ISN'T RIGHT AND SOMETIMES WHAT'S RIGHT ISN'T WHAT'S BEST.'- Words of Jack wisdom.

"Nice hair-do." Ollie says in between bites of his sandwich.

"Funny." is Yankee's only response as he takes Brinly's seat placing a pistol on the table aimed in Ollie's general direction while picking off Brinly's plate and leisurely making himself at home.

Ollie watches Yankee closely while in the background signs of life appear out of Barley who's rolling over with a confused look on his face.

"I couldn't believe it when I got the call. The Time Broker's card had been pulled. Naturally I didn't waste a minute tracking you down. Aren't you curious why?" Yankee asks but is disappointed by the Broker's answer.

"Not really, I'm sure you're here to avenge some loved one who probably got killed in the line of fire. How close am I, Sport?" Ollie retorts before taking a sip of his cola.

"Close enough." Yankee mutters while cocking the hammer back on his gun before adding, "Keep your hands flat on the table, I won't repeat myself."

"You know I've waited a lifetime for this moment right here. I'll savor this memory above all others, you have that honor." Yankee says with a little tremble of excitement showing in the shaking of his hand.

"My Uncle was part of the force sent to bring you in twenty years ago. They wore this suit to prevent you from robbing their time from them. They were going to change the world with that watch, change the Jacks and how they policed the supernatural. Marked as saviors by the young Jacks leading the uproar my Uncle set off on his mission…He never came back." Yankee says and a light flashes in Ollie's head as he remembers where he's seen the short guy before.

"Awe those clowns, yeah I remember them. Maybe he joined the circus? P.S. Those suits didn't operate at capacity out in the field." Ollie chuckles aloud causing Yankee's face to seethe from the comment causing the gun in his hand to tremble as Yankee fights to hold back the turmoil within him.

"You killed him!" Yankee shouts finally giving in to his rage as he starts to slightly wave his gun in the shape for infinity as he softly says aloud, "Eenie, Meenie, Miniee…"

"Actually it was him." Ollie chimes in stalling Yankee Jack's count. Yankee pauses only slightly at Ollie's statement, watching the grin grow upon his face, before realizing why his would be victim is smiling.

… BANG! …

"MOE!" Barley says and fires a single shot at point blank range into the back of Yankee's skull. The splatter of brains and blood cover the wall as Yankee's head drops into Brinly's plate causing her food to cascade off of the table.

The waitress comes rushing up from checking on the non responsive woman in the bathroom to see Barley calmly standing over the dead body of Yankee Jack while aiming a pistol at Ollie.

"OH MY GOD! Who are they?!" the waitress screams out at Ollie causing Barley to shift his focus slightly to put two in her chest.

…BANG-BANG…

"Ok the fun and games are over. Let's go Broker." Barley says with a sinister smile.

Ollie only slightly grins as he ignites the Chronometer freezing the wild eyed gun man in his tracks. Barley had only looked away for a split second but that's all the time Ollie needed to twist his dials to the precise settings to pause Barley in his tracks.

"Hello Barley I see time's been unkind to you, proof there is a God I guess. You know I thought it would be a shame if your buddy just died never knowing it was you who actually killed his uncle, your own partner and friend. Bet he loved to learn that you were the Rat that fed vital Intel to your elder Jacks giving them the advantage over the young Jacks in The War of the Twelves." Ollie says as Barley interrupts, "Friends? NEVER!"

"I had considered letting you live, to send a message back to all your superiors you understand... But you shot the waitress. It's true she was a little salty at best but I know she didn't deserve getting to have her last thoughts being 'why?', as she stared at your ugly mug. Now I got to cleanse the building of any evidence and now we got to find somewhere else to eat. Jeez you Jacks could fuck up a wet dream I swear it." Ollie chuckles out as he sips his cola with an evil grin of his own.

"We?" is Barley's last word as the Chronometer arcs to life in a picturesque glow of blue light as time blasts Barley, Yankee, and the rest of the diner to little more than a memory. Ollie hops up holding his leftovers and strolls through the now hollowed out hull of a restaurant to make sure Brinly is alright.

"Brinly? Brinly are you ok?!" Ollie asks through the locked door to the sound of crickets so he asks again, "Brinly? I'm coming in."

Ollie warns her one more time now worried to death that the Jacks were just a distraction to something worst. Raring back Ollie busts through the door startling Brinly who had fallen asleep so bad she falls off the toilet.

“Fuck sakes Ollie! You scared me.” Brinly says as she scrambles to her feet while slamming the door to the bathroom.

“Sorry, sorry I was concerned, I had some trouble with a couple of Jack offs and things got a little out of hand. Not to rush but we need to leave. There’s a better joint on down the road.” is all Ollie says as he waits for his driver to wash her hands before slipping out the back to avoid the mess. …

Chapter Five

The Erased

The last rays of the sun are quickly dissipating from the sky making way for the bright and glitzy glow of Las Vegas come to life as two weary travelers feel relieved at stopping the car for a while.

"I don't know about you Ollie but I've gone as far as I'm going to go I don't care who's chasing us. I want a shower, a hot meal, and some rest." Brinly announces as they come up on the infamous Flamingo Hotel and Casino.

"Keep going, I got a guy at the Horseshoe who owes me one. We can stay there." Ollie says with a grin as they both gaze out at the city of casinos that seems to just keep growing.

It isn't long before Brin, exhausted from the drive parks her car and takes a long stretch before they make their way inside the world famous Horseshoe Casino.

Brinly holds onto Ollie as he makes his way back to the poker room to see his old friend. Brin is amazed at the character of the place as she gazes back and fourth from one exciting win to another she imagines it's what a saloon in the old west would be like.

It gets tight as spectators crowd around a No Limit table in the poker room for a big hand in progress. "The action here is always incredible." Ollie turns to Brin and says while adding, "Hold on." before squeezing through the crowd like thread through the eye of a needle.

It felt like forever inside the crowd of excitement and cheering Brinly thought to herself when she hears someone say, "THE KID'S GOT HIM ALL IN AND DEAD TO ONE OUT!"

Suddenly they popped out the other side with Ollie not even looking at the game in progress having set his sights in on his target. But a voice from the past brings his gaze to the game and the man who happens to be the one all in and way behind.

"Oliver my boy, you haven't aged a day." Johnny says as he patiently awaits the final outcome of this epic duel he's carried on for weeks with this young kid named Ungar.

"Clean living my friend. I see you're still burning the candle at both ends, looks like you could use a little time." Ollie says while the hand continues to play out as the dealer exposes the turn card that's no help leaving only one card to go before Ollie's pal is felted.

"Since you're asking, I could use an Ace on the river." Johnny calmly says with the slightest of smiles appearing on his stoic and weathered face as the dealer burns and starts to turn the river card.

"Seriously I'm no miracle worker John, that's your department." Ollie slyly says as he takes his hand off his Chronometer with a wink to his old pal.

That's when the whole place erupts in excitement and disbelief at the one outer that just hit the river saving Johnny's life. The enormous fortune destined for the young phenom who's battled Johnny tooth and nail is now being slowly pushed to the old man.

The kid takes it in stride with a satisfying smile growing across his face saying, "Nice hand John." before standing up for a stretch and a smoke while telling his backer to reload him with a single gesture.

"And the legend continues." Ollie says as he pats Johnny on the shoulder before turning to head to his original destination with Brinly gripped tightly to his arm.

"I can't believe you just did that." Brinly softly says as she nudges Ollie about using the Chronometer to ensure an Ace hit the river. Brinly saw it all as she was hanging on to Ollie when he paused time to switch out the river card without anyone noticing.

"Always look out for your pals." is all Ollie says as he sneaks up behind the Horseshoe's card room manager. Ollie sticks his hand into his old friend's back like a pistol startling the gentleman only slightly before saying, "A minute for your thoughts."

Slowly turning around the man is already grinning from ear to ear, "Ollie! Wow how long has it been? Man, how are you? Haven't aged a day I see, Lucky Bastard." The man rattles off like an old jukebox that just won't quit till he catches a glance of Brinly causing the record to skip.

After a quick introduction to Mr. Jim Savage the poker room manager and self proclaimed provider of fantasies here at the Horseshoe, Brinly sits down in a chair out of pure exhaustion.

Ollie walks over to a waitress giving her a $100 dollar bill while whispering something and nodding in Brinly's direction.

"Ollie I wish I knew you were coming in, we've got zero availability tonight. The whole strip is booked up solid. You know there's always room at my place if you need to lay low for a bit. But give me a second, let me a call or two." Jim says as his grabs the phone dialing up one of his most reliable connects in times of need before adding as he hangs up the phone, "They're going to call back."

The waitress returns with four shots of Tennessee whiskey and a cup of fresh coffee. "Here you go Broker. It's good to see you again." the waitress says with a wink as she offers Brinly the coffee. Brinly chooses the whiskey instead, leaving the hot cup of Joe for Ollie's friend.

Suddenly the phone rings back and Jim snatches it off the ringer in hopes of some good news.

"I see, alright, yes I'm quite positive that will be just fine. Sara you're an angel, I owe you... oh I see, yes you can count me in on a private viewing thank you very much." Jim says and hastily hangs up the phone.

"Ok I got you a room." Jim says.

"Where?" is Ollie's response.

"It's the Honeymoon suite." Jim tries to sweeten the deal knowing in his heart that Ollie will never go for it.

"Where is it at?" Ollie asks with a little more frustration in his tone.

"It's at the Nugget." Jim says and Brinly chimes in, "That sounds perfect."

“No, no that’s ok Jim, I’d rather stay here.” Ollie says as he begins scanning the check in area.

“Gotcha’” Ollie says and quickly points out the couple to Jim who calls the front desk getting the names of the cute old couple that just slowly wheeled their way over to the slots after getting checked in.

Brinly takes a moment to awe from the sign on the back of their wheelchairs that simply reads ‘Just Married’ as Ollie slips up to the old couple with the deal of a century. Brin watches curiously as Ollie talks with them for only a moment before tapping the Chronometer causing Ollie and the old couple to disappear in a flash from the current time stream. …

Inside the time bubble the old couple sits amazed at how everything is frozen in time.

“Have you ever seen anything quite like it Earl?” the little blue haired lady says as she stares out at all the people who look like mannequin.

Ollie gives them a moment to take it in before he asks, “If you could do it all over again, what would you change?”

The couple gazes into each others eyes longing for the one thing they lack over everything else before answering.

"I'd find her sooner just to love her longer." the old man grunts out in a coarse and gravelly tone while still pulling the handle on the one armed bandit that’s currently frozen like everything else.

Ollie smiles at the answer knowing he had them right where he wanted them.

"Well I do believe it's your lucky day." Ollie says and gains the old couples full attention.

"What if I offered you all the time in the world to be together, to relive your life as a young newly wed couple with no need for wheelchairs or blood pressure medicine, to have a lifetime together frozen at the perfect age? Would you take it?" Ollie asks with a shy grin on his face.

"And for this act of generosity I'm guessing all you'll need in return are our eternal souls, right?" Earl says with a load of sarcasm and disbelief.

"No actually the only thing that I will require is your accommodations for the night." Ollie chuckles as he sees both of their eyes grow to the size of saucer plates before Earl's wife blurts out, "Sold!"

And in a flash the deal was done. …

It only took a second from Brinly's point of view, 'they disappeared only to reappear a second later.'

The old couple was gone and in their place stands an awkwardly dressed young couple no older than twenty. The newly weds can't take their eyes off each other as long dormant desires hit them both like a thunder bolt.

Their grey hairs are gone forever changed back to their natural brown hues. Both stands with their postures from their youth, no more hunched back no more wheelchairs.

“Actually, we may need that room for a moment or two.” the young lady so vibrant and voluptuous says while barely containing herself in this public place.

“I can do you one better than that.” Ollie says as he leads them over to where his friend and Brinly are standing some what in shock at what they’ve seen.

“Make it the Honeymoon suite and I’ll call it even, consider it a wedding present from me.” Ollie says with a wink making him cool as a cucumber as Jim excitedly shouts, “Done!”

“Thank you so much Mr.?” the young lady says waiting to find out this good Samaritans name as she hands him their key.

“The Time Broker, you can call me the Time Broker. Stay out of trouble you crazy kids.” Ollie says with a sly smile as Jim takes them over to meet his friend at the Nugget.

“Wow all that for a room here? We could’ve just walked over there.” Brinly says with a yawn as they now walk toward the elevators that lead to their room for the night.

“Yeah we could’ve. But if I’m going to be in Vegas, the Shoe’s the only place to be.” Ollie says as he hits the button to signal the elevator.

“You know that was amazing, right? You just gave that couple a brand new lease on life.” Brinly says as the doors open and they step into the awaiting elevator.

“Maybe, but I doubt it’ll be all rainbows and love songs come tomorrow.” Ollie says as the elevator doors close.

Ollie's reference is to the only draw back of instantly regaining your youth, which is no one who knew you yesterday will believe who you are today.

Brinly smiles at his comment with a look like she's ready to hit the showers and that's just what she does as soon as their in the room.

Ollie's alone now for the moment, alone with his thoughts as the shower runs so hot from the bathroom residual steam creeps up behind him.

'What am I thinking bringing her into this as deep as I have, without so much as a thought of how much further we'll have to go, or even the risk that's included?' fills Ollie's mind like an avalanche as he wanders the room truly exhausted in his own right. Ollie slides the curtain open to admire the lights.

"Only in Vegas." Ollie says with a smile as the shower cuts off.

Brinly cracks the seal of the bathroom door and emerges through the mist wearing only a T-shirt of her old university her hair glistens in the light. And with a glance Ollie forgets everything he was thinking about as Brinly fills his gaze.

"Does it always do that?" Brinly coyly asks with a nod to the Chronometer that's spinning around wildly like a carousal in freefall.

"What can I say, you get me all wound up." Ollie slyly replies before Brinly watches him go from fully clothed to damp and wearing just a towel in the blink of an eye.

Brinly just grins at what awaits as she flips off the lights to what's bound to be an interesting night. …

Another time…

Hours later.

At another place…

In a downtown Chicago skyscraper.

Within the infamous headquarters to the secret society known only by the name the Happy Jack's, it's their American branch hid under the banner of the well known and honored Jackson, Wolf, & Associates.

A set of brass elevator doors open to reveal a young woman with a mousy posture holding a stack of files. She quietly gazes down the long hallway that's been untouched by time as she focuses on a single door made of stained glass.

Stepping out just as the elevator doors begin to close, causes her to stumble and drop her arm full of files after she lunged a little harder than normal trying to beat the elevators automatic action.

Hurriedly she gathers the files up and makes her way to the door pausing only for a moment to gain composure before knocking.

She only knocks once before entering the penthouse office of the head of the Jacks. The décor is a flawless peek into the classic art deco movement of the fifties as a voice from the shadows asks, "Report."

"They made contact with the Broker at..." the young woman announces but is cut off by her newly re-crowned boss.

(It happened in a flash and the whole organization has been reeling from the sudden shift in management since she miraculously reappeared looking like the twenty year old version of herself.)

"They?" is all the woman asks as she reaches out for the files in her mousy assistants hands.

"Yes 'they'. There was a rogue agent in play, he intercepted our own. There was another car in the parking lot besides Barley's. Both were heavily damaged by time I'm guessing it belonged to the rogue." She tells her boss who fails to seem surprised.

"And the Broker, he got away, correct?" the boss asks without any surprise in her tone.

"Yes he did. Far as they can tell the two Jacks wound up in a fight that ravaged the diner ending with both of their retirements, the cook's card was also pulled. I've done some snooping around and it seems the rogue agent was contacted from this building. Give me a few hours and I'll find the source." The young woman tells her boss with a smile as any good agent would.

"Excellent job Jackie, before you locate the source I need you to run down to sub-level six and bring me the vitals of our latest participant." She tells the mousy young lady.

"Isn't that a job for the handlers, Mam?" the young lady asks with a touch of concern as to where exactly she's been asked to go. She's heard the rumors of sub-level six, there's even a running joke around the office about what it takes to get level six clearance and none of them are good.

"Well today it's a... What's your title again? Oh yeah that's right you're an Agent of the Jacks, so as an agent it sounds like it's a Jackie job, today." the boss responds as she stops shuffling the files around on her desk to give her full attention to her newest thorn in her side.

"I've requested my information. Now go and fetch it or be replaced immediately! It's in cell number nine." are the woman's final words said in the harshest tone a person could muster.

And away the agent went scurrying off into the shadows of the building like a mouse after a piece of cheese.

The woman who gave the order picks up her phone soon as the elevators close and dials the number to the security office on level six.

"Lockdown all exits on your level and deactivate cell number nine after my secretary arrives… No, no just do it and take a break… Yes, there will be a containment breach, so perhaps use your time wisely and prepare accordingly for GOD'S SAKE!" She slams the phone down before taking a moment to make note that she'll need a new assistant from here on as she drops all the information about the incident involving Yankee Jack in the shredder.

She pulls out an old picture of Ollie and herself. It's from the old days of the Capone era Chicago. Ollie's smile is infectious, frozen in the frame of the photo, his arm around her as they pose to capture the moment.

"I'm going to pay you back Oliver, just you wait." She says while longingly looking at the photo with a tear in her eye and vengeance in her voice. …

Back across the country after an amazing night and now an uninterrupted breakfast Ollie and Brinly have arrived at the fork in the road out in the Mojave Desert when the question is asked?

"So where to now Ollie?" Brinly wonders aloud as they stand deep within the canyons just outside of Vegas with their now present path blocked by an enormous red rock.

Brinly hears Ollie whistling an old timey song and a bad feeling hits her from the pit of her stomach.

"Are you whistling 'Big Rock Candy Mountain'?" Brinly asks as she now looks up at how high it is to the top of this miniature mountain Ollie is staring at as if he's fixing to scale it.

"Up and over... is that what that song was called?" Ollie says with a slight grin of sarcasm before taking the first step up finding the necessary foot holds from the instructions in the book to find the cavern of the Erased.

Brinly takes a moment to stare up the sheer rock face before grunting, "Perfect." and then they climb and climb. Brinly is surprised at how easy they transverse the landscape even with a hand drawn map littered with scribbled details about how to get to the cavern.

It isn't long before they reach the top, excited and out of breath, Brinly spins around to take in the view stopping the instant she completes the circle.

"Wow what a view." Brinly says while taking it all in. She notices as she gulps her canteen that Ollie hasn't even took the time to look up as he continues to stare at the map his father made for him.

"Which way now?" Brin curiously asks while watching as Ollie pulls his nose out of the book to get his bearings. After studying the directions one last time Ollie gazes out into the mesmerizing horizon briefly with his arm outstretched ending at the tip of his index finger then turns 180 degrees.

It's like magic as the entrance to the cavern of the Erased seems to materialize out of the rocks like it was dying to be seen.

"There's the door." Ollie says with a chuckle while slightly tilting his head to gauge their distance from the cave that sits at the bottom of the next ravine before reaching for the canteen.

Brinly just shakes her head at how far is left, she was hoping the door would be at the top of the climb but it looks like they aren't even halfway there.

"We'll be lucky to be there before sunset." Brinly says as she slowly creeps closer to the edge trying her best not to slip.

"Maybe but I have another idea." Ollie says as he takes two steps back behind Brinly before lunging off the top taking her with him. You could measure the distance they fell by her blood curdling scream. And at the very last second just before impact time stands still. Brinly is still screaming while yet to realize they've stopped falling.

"Brin! Brinly calm down!" Ollie shouts gaining her attention.

"We're not dead oh thank God we're not dead. What the FUCK OLLIE! That was far from funny! Why didn't you use that on the way up?" Brinly shouts as she climbs down from her position with Ollie giving the most obvious answer, "Gravity." adding fuel to the fire before he tries to calm her down.

"I'm sorry, you're right, that wasn't funny. It's just that I didn't think you would jump off a cliff with me and I needed us to be close enough to be in the Chronometer's reach before we hit the ground." Ollie chuckles only slightly before shutting it down from the look Brin has given him.

"Ok from this point forward no surprises, cross my heart." Ollie says and gets a momentary chuckle out of Brin before her scowl returns.

In a flash Brinly forgets about being mad as she now looks at the cave entrance that's a lot larger than she thought, "Wow that's got to be forty feet tall!"

"So tell me about this Erased?" Brinly says as she reaches into her pack pulling out a bright flashlight and taking Ollie by the hand before stepping into the dark and mysterious cave.

The cavern is amazing as the ground seems to shimmer in the light like nothing Brin has ever seen. There's something else too, it's like this cave was made by a large bolt of lightning from the gods' or something. It's kind of a unbelievable feeling is Brinly's best way to describe it.

"The Erased is a myth, a monster of legend. It is said that he was once a God but was banished here. He's better known as his alias the Grim Reaper. So if we find him don't be startled by his appearance. My Dad briefly told me about his experience with the Erased. In my Father's journal there is another tale. My Dad even considered him a friend." Ollie rattles off as they make their way into the inner parts of the large winding cavern.

"AND!" Brinly urges impatiently waiting for the story she knows is about to come.

"Eons ago there were deities that roamed the existence never restrained by the dimensions or the realities that they stepped through. They created new life on planets and destroyed entire cosmoses wherever they went. Their will was reality. And the Erased was once one of those deities.

He was a creator who loved what he did it's just that he hated who he had to follow. The Deity at the head of the line was a deity named Corvan Sin. Corvan's the true definition of a monster. They walked in a single file line and any deity in front of you was considered your elder, it's kind of crazy." Ollie pauses as he freezes in his tracks nearly falling down a deep dark crevice in the floor of the cave.

Leaping over it Ollie firmly grips Brinly's waist as she lands just to ensure she doesn't fall before continuing down their path.

"Anyways, the Erased grew frustrated with following Corvan's path and planned a new route for them all. The Erased created a powerful pendent enchanted with abilities like none before it with the purpose of erasing Corvan from their existence. But Corvan being Corvan knew of the plan and attacked the creator using his own device against him. Erasing him from the existence he had always known and banishing him to this dimension forever. And over the centuries the Erased befriended many people along his path. Amongst his friends was my father who the Erased helped by giving my Dad the ore from this cave, which my father used to create the Chronometer. My Dad kept a journal with the hand written accounts of the stories the Erased told him over the years. I had read several of the stories without completely comprehending them thanks to the missing pages that gave the location plus the much needed text to unlock the stories." Ollie finishes the quick sum up about who they are seeking out.

They notice signs of mining throughout the first hundred yards or so and then it abruptly stops as if something ran the miners off. From that point after the cave glistens in a strange and other worldly way as they continued their decent.

The climb isn't quite strenuous but combined with the two earlier ones Ollie and Brin are starting to feel this one. They're about fifty feet down when a set of white hot glowing eyes catches Brinly's attention. Anyone else's initial reaction would be to scream, but not Brin. This ain't her first time in uncharted waters.

"Ollie, OLLIE!" Brin quietly chirps down to gain his attention.

Ollie stops moving to hear the movement of the set of eyes he's now locked onto. But having some unsure footing caused a large rock to fall down the throat of the cave sounding like a giant bowling ball wreaking havoc over and over again.

The echoing chaos caused the set of eyes to disappear into the darkness of an off shoot of the narrow cave. Looking around Ollie finds a set of stairs carved out of the strange rock that seems to form this cave system.

Taking the stairs the two rushes to catch up to the monster that vanished into the pitch black.

"Ollie, hold on do we even know what it is we're chasing. Who's to say it's not waiting on us around anyone of these dark corners?!" Brinly blurts out seemingly causing Ollie to stop in his tracks. But in fact he halted at what he saw before him around the next corner.

"It's magnificent!" Ollie says flashing the light across the unexplainable place. Brinly scrambles up to see for herself, and wow what an understatement as Brinly bares witness to a carved out cathedral with several corridors that lead to God knows where.

"Hello! Hello! There's no need to be afraid! We mean you no harm!" Brinly shouts out causing a slew of noise to echo around the dwelling.

So after a moment of silence Ollie whispers, "Let's just try hello."

"Who are you?" a voice older than time calls out from the darkness.

"My name is Oliver, Oliver..." Ollie starts to say but is interrupted by the voice.

"Pendulum, you're Oliver Pendulum, son of Bartholomew Pendulum, the creator of the Chronometer. You sound just like him." the voice says as he pokes his head out from around the corner of a long corridor just beside Ollie and Brin.

"I would apologize about my appearance but there's nothing I can do about it, be careful and try not to touch me, my skin is quite toxic to most people. Come in come in, please make yourselves at home." the Erased says as he flips a switch and the entire place lights up like a tree at Christmas.

And every corner in this place is packed full of items from the priceless range all the way to the 'what is that' range.

One of the more unique items is the remnants of an old salon from the old west days including the bar, tables, and even a fancy chandelier but the evidence of his treasure trove proves too much as it spills out over the dance floor first hidden from their view.

"Wow can you say hoarder? Are you the Erased?" Brinly says and asks quietly as she walks around admiring the collection. Ollie notices a slight sigh in the skeleton before he answers.

"Yes, that is one of the names I am known by." the Erased says with his head obviously tilted.

"Well you know that's so impersonal, how about Archie?" Ollie states drawing the full attention of the Erased which he's guessing is a look of confusion.

"Archie?" the Erased says as he walks behind his bar to retrieve a vintage bottle of bourbon and three dusty glasses, "I like Archie."

"Archie I'm here because there's something my Dad mentioned in his journal that you made for him? I think it can contain Corvan that's how we came to be here now. Can you think of what it could've been?" Ollie asks while trying not to stare at the skeleton he's currently having a conversation with though it's hard not too due to the enchanted glow of the eyes of the Erased.

Archie stays motionless for only a split second before jumping up and rushing out of the room. Brin and Ollie hear the crashing sound of what must have been a slight cave in somewhere within the mountain of stuff. Archie pops back in holding a set of drawings done by Ollie's Dad.

"Bart spent months here designing the device he called the Chronometer using a set of his hand drawn schematics, sculpting every little piece of it by hand. We grew close and he came to visit me over the years helping to add to the collection, that section of trunks and containers is his, well yours." Archie explains as he points out a whole section of the cave neatly stacked up against the wall looking untouched for centuries.

Unsurprised at the size of his Father's hoarded treasure, It's not the first one Ollie has found in his long lived life. Ollie goes straight for the original sketches of his watch while Brinly can't help but to peek inside one of the trunks.

"Ollie this thing is full of gravel?" Brinly says as she scoops up a hand full before pouring them back out and into the trunk to show him.

With only the slightest of smiles appearing on Ollie's face that's presently glued to the art in his hands he responds, "That's not gravel."

"Then what are they?" Brin asks as she takes a look at the last one in her hand.

"Those my dear are diamonds, uncut diamonds. I'm sure they're part of a fifth century treasure my Pops acquired in his travels." Ollie says as he looks closely at The Chronometer realizing there's one notch left, room for one more dial.

"Oh my God I feel like I'm in the Count of Monte Cristo." Brinly abruptly says as she sits in awe at what she's seen.

"Bart said this was the key to his problems, the answer to his prayers. It's the schematic of the last dial left to add to the Chronometer. Once it's in place you will be able to unlock a new set of controls including the ability to contain Corvan within the Chronometer theoretically speaking of course. I was finishing it when Bart suddenly left one night with the instructions that he would return in a month with you. He never returned." Archie says as he hands over the last drawing to Ollie.

"Great that sounds perfect Archie, now where is this key?" Ollie asks as he's looked over all the drawings enough to have them memorized forever. Now all he wants is the actual dial, in the flesh so to speak.

"They were like an infestation. Swarming in and picking my wonderful treasure clean. All you see here is what I have left." Archie says as Brinly looks around the enormous collection thinking he could stand a spring cleaning.

"You had more than this in here?" Brinly surprisingly says as she looks around again to take it all in.

"This is only a tenth of what this cavern once held. And when they got done with the artifacts gold and jewels they started mining the ore from the walls. It took me a long time to rid this place of those parasites. Your Dad's key was one of the artifacts taken." Archie says in an apologetic tone as Ollie seems to just sit there frozen in time.

Brinly comes over and puts a sympathetic hand on Ollie's shoulder. She realizes this has been a long time coming for Ollie and every time they get close it's like the rug gets pulled out from under them.

"Of course it was...You wouldn't happen to know which way these parasites went with our goods, would you." Ollie asks already knowing who the parasites are since it was his torn out pages that led the Jacks here fifty plus years ago.

"I know where they took it all, but I can't show you. Once people notice me the police show up, then it progresses from there, till I'm facing off with an army of tanks. So no thanks kid I'll be fine right here." Archie says as he leans back to catch a glimpse of himself in the mirror before sighing aloud.

"What if we made a deal, you take me to the exact spot you last saw our stuff and..." Ollie starts to proposition but Archie interrupts.

"And you'll what exactly?" Archie barks out with his arms crossed thinking there's no way this kid could give Archie what he really wants, it's unobtainable.

"I've got an acquaintance who owes me a rather large favor or two. He works in the field of molecular biology. He's your best bet at really seeing your face again. And boy does he love an unsolvable problem, you would definitely qualify." Ollie pops backs with a grin as it now seems that the skeleton is frozen in place.

"So what do you say, you in?" Ollie says with a chuckle as he reaches out to shake Archie's hand.

"I'm in, but we still got to get me there without being noticed." Archie says without a clue as to how long it'll take only traveling at night.

"Don't worry I've got an idea." Brinly snickers as she wildly lunges into her backpack like she has the solution to Archie's problem.

It's the sound of a can rattling toward all three of them that pulls Brinly's attention out of the bag with panty hose in one hand and her canteen in the other.

BOOM!!!!!!

A loud explosion rips through the air followed by a constant spewing sound as knockout gas engulfs the cavern. …

Chapter Six

Rogues Gallery

Hours later, out on the open road of the sundrenched dessert.

It's blazing hot! The bright UV rays are relentlessly cascading down the crispy red back of the tired and confused Brinly Rachel Blevins.

Brin's been walking down the side of this old two lane blacktop for what feels like a month without seeing a single car. Her last memory was of them, they took him.

She tried to give chase but the gas knocked her out or she fainted again, at this point Brin really has no idea. The only thing she's sure of is where she woke up which was right in the middle of the fucking desert. Also she's parched. …

Not too far behind her.

Driving down the highway as fast as he can the Erased now preferring to be called Archie feels invigorated as he rushes to catch up with the kidnappers. Oliver Pendulum promised to help him find a bit of normal in this life and get reconnected with the world without dealing with all the screams from his appearance.

That's reason enough to leave the cave. The car he took is as hot as the sun. Archie found it at the Red Rock National Park entrance and figured why the hell not, though he did throw a little makeshift disguise together so as not to stick out like a sore thumb to any passer bys.

It isn't long before he slows to a stop as he comes upon the first grizzly sight, having no idea there will be more.

The armored ex-military vehicle has been torn to pieces drowned in blood and still smolders from the recent fire. There's no way to I.D. anybody causes that's all they are, just bodies. All their heads and some shoulders have been cleanly taken off by the looks of it; an insanely large beast with seriated knives for teeth and armor piercing claws for …claws.

Archie finds signs of a shootout and the beast's bloody paw prints fade out only a half a mile away from the wreck. Though they start back up a couple of miles later where Archie finds the second wreck, it's a mirror image of the last except for one small silver whistle Archie finds in the wreckage. He knows now these corpses are the Jacks, that's who took his new friends. What he doesn't know is what killed the Jacks?

After passing the third wreck identical to the others in distance apart and destruction Archie prepares to find the next wreckage as the odometer clicks of another half mile.

Nothing, no wreck no bodies just plain old nothing, that is until Archie stretches his gaze out toward the horizon. With a sigh of relief he takes off gaining the attention of the wandering hitchhiker out in the middle of nowhere.

A large smile grows upon Brinly's face as she watches her own car slow to a stop, behind the wheel is a skeleton wearing pantyhose over his head in a poor attempt to conceal the fact that he's a skeleton.

"Archie, how'd you know this was my car?" Brinly asks with a carefree tone of relief to finally get out of the sun.

"Intuition young lady, how did you escape the beast and where is Ollie?" Archie retorts not revealing the blind luck he had of knowing this was her car. Brinly rummages around in the back seat till she pulls out an enormous canteen. Brinly tilts it back allowing the glorious water trapped inside to flow all over her face and down her neck as she gulps it down till her thirst is quenched.

"I'm not sure? I don't know how I got here, last thing I remember is people taking Ollie and I gave chase till the gas overtook me. Where are we going?" Brinly responds as she looks at Archie's appearance knowing they were going to have to do a better job of concealment, though she has to admit that it was nice to actually see the outline of Archie's face through the thin texture of the pantyhose.

"Those people were the Happy Jacks and judging by their trajectory I know exactly where they're going, Chicago." Archie says as the wind from his current speed blows through the speeding car.

"Well if we're going to be traveling buddies then we got to do something about that disguise." Brinly chuckles as she pulls her backpack into reach and starts going through it searching for clothes.

"What's wrong with my disguise?" Archie asks as he looks at his shady appearance in the rearview mirror.

"Nothing if you were planning on looking like a skeleton that's dressed to rob the corner market." Brinly says as she pulls out a sun dress.

"And you think that's less suspicious? I should've got to you sooner." Archie responds concerned that his passenger has gotten sunstroke.

"The dress is for me, you'll take a little more panache." Brinly says with a smile, already having an idea or two of how to deal with Archie's mingling problem. …

Across the country tucked away nicely within the Windy City.

Ollie sits at the Jacks interrogation table with his hands cuffed behind his back still unable to access his Chronometer. He's never felt more trapped in his life, well that is if you discount everything after he put on the Chronometer. It's a gift and a curse as most things are.

There are three Jacks in military grab, locked and loaded in the corners of the room with their sights set on the Broker. Ollie's lovingly named them the Goon Squad for kicks, steel toed kicks it seemed. Sadly he's taken the beating of a lifetime due mainly to that mouth of his, if only Ollie knew when to shut up.

The Goon Squad's posture changes as the sound of foot steps ring through the room from just outside the door. Sounding like a grizzly bear in combat boots Ollie can't wait to barely see whoever it is.

The door sounds like its being ripped apart at the seams from the strength of the monster behind it as it opens.

"Holy Shit!" Ollie thinks out loud and is honestly shocked at this monster of a man's size, he's almost unnatural like a Sasquatch that shaved and called himself Jack.

"He's definitely the missing link." Ollie thinks as he hears the behemoths low growl while he chews on his cigar.

"Where's the monster?" the man asks as he blows a cloud of stale smoke into Ollie's face.

"You're shitting me right?! I'm staring right at you. How did you even fit through the door?" Ollie chirps back as he vaguely remembers just who he's looking at from all the stories he's been told through the years from his old and strangely absent friend and agent Samantha Hawthorn.

"That's funny Broker. It's good to see they haven't smashed your sense of humor." the man says as he swaps his cigar from one side of his mouth to his other.

"How could they, look how they're dressed." Ollie rattles off as he notices someone slip into the shadows behind the beast of a man asking questions.

"Wait I remember you now, yeah that's it. You're the ...Lumber Jack!" Ollie chuckles after pausing momentarily for the suspense of it.

Lumber Jack steps closer, posturing to hit Ollie for his continued chatter when Ollie interrupts, "No really I've heard about the Jack they experimented on and turned into a monster just to take down their tainted hero. What was his name again?"

"Don't you speak it!" the Jack growls louder than before.

"The myth, the legend, your mentor, your confidant, the one the only Hue..." Ollie mutters but before he could finish he takes the full force of a fist the size of a brick–o-block, THUUUDDD!

"Damn what a lick! Huelet teach you that?" Ollie smarts off spilling blood all over the floor from the punch still not learning his lesson while the Lumber Jack prepares another for the Broker saying the forgotten name.

"Whoa, whoa, whoa, you keep hitting me like that and you're gonna have a lot of explaining to do when the boss gets here. Just go ahead and ask your question." Ollie says referring to who he's guessing is pulling the strings and his guess is confirmed just moments later.

"I already did." the Jack angrily states as he starts to swing again but is abruptly halted by the voice hiding behind him.

"See what I mean, I'm now damaged thanks to... Who are you again?" Ollie mocks losing his memory just for the continued mental anguish it gives the Jack.

"That's enough, take a break Carver." a familiar voice tells her agent as she slips out of the shadows behind the monster of a man revealing herself to her prisoner, "Hello lover."

"Wow it didn't take you long to fall back into your old ways, did it?" Ollie says with a tad more zeal as he stares at the now ageless beauty of Ms. Sophia Sincliar Renault.

"You can thank yourself for that, Broker." Sophia announces as she lightly brushes the backside of her hand down Ollie's bloody cheek, "All I wanted was to die, to be rid of you and the torment you've brought to my heart."

"Oh Sweetie I'm sure you've realized by now... that you can thank yourself for that... if you haven't then give it some time, you got plenty." Ollie says with a wink that looked like anything other than the gesture he had in mind thanks to the beating he's taken.

"Poor little Ollie, the Time Broker, eyes swollen shut, blood trickling from just about everywhere, and still you insist on denying the truth." Sophia says as she takes a damp washcloth and gently wipes away the blood on Ollie's face.

"Laying all jokes aside because I know you'll never stop unless I have you're complete attention and I intend to gain just that." Sophia says as she slides Ollie's chair back just enough to slip her leg over and straddle the once love of her life. Ollie's so exhausted he doesn't even have the strength to fight her advances. Sophia slowly draws closer before gently placing her lips on his.

"Where is your monster?" Sophia softly whispers as she sensually grinds on her prisoner like she's done many times before back in the Capone era of Chicago, back when it felt like they were the only two in the world that mattered. …

They were in love once many, many moons ago. It was a different time with different rules. And even amongst all the chaos of the world they existed in, they found each other. That is until the day Sophia's father and head of the Jacks organization Sullivan Sinclair made the call to apprehend the Time Broker. Sullivan wanted the Chronometer for himself knowing full in well that that's all it would take to keep society safe from the monsters from now on out.

Sophia had to do something so she made a choice and has had to live with the regret everyday since. It broke her heart the night she left, the way she left the place. Sophia knew what it would do to her love, but she knew it was better than what her father had in store.

"Keep going you'll find it." Ollie sarcastically says as he rocks his head back like he's in heaven and as mad as he is at Sophia there's a part of him that longs for her even now. Love always leaves its mark.

Sophia starts to undo her shirt button by button as Ollie can't help but to watch. Sophia was a specimen to be adored back in the day and now in the present day too.

Suddenly Ollie's head cocks to one side as he notices what she's wearing around her neck. Ollie stares at it for a long time before realizing it's the last ring to his Chronometer hanging on a small gold chain.

"Do I have your attention now, lover." Sophia says with a smirk as she slips off of him while buttoning up her shirt.

"Now where is the monster?" Sophia asks as she takes the necklace off gently placing it on the table. Sophia gives a leisurely snap of her fingers causing the Lumber Jack to jump into action.

The Jack retrieves a large hammer from a box under the table used to persuade the truth out of the werewolves during similar interrogations. And now with a heinous grin on his ugly face the Lumber Jack postures over the prize that Ollie is desperate to obtain.

"Listen, don't do this." Ollie says in a more worried tone than the sarcastic one he's had throughout his interrogation.

"Sophia I truly don't know what you're talking about, don't do this, please." Ollie says as he watches the behemoth swing full force. The impact sends a burst of light from the sparks causing Ollie to light up in anger much like the burst.

"You stupid motherfucker! I promise you the slowest of deaths when I get out of this!" Ollie shouts at the fact they are trying to destroy his only opportunity to stop the deity Corvan Sin and end his unrelenting nightmare.

"Don't you get it Broker, you're never getting out. Time catches up to everyone and finally it's caught you." Lumber Jack tells Ollie as he hits the small ring again and again but the harder he hits it's the brighter it glows.

"It's a massive and amazing animal I must admit, plus the first of it's kind as far as we know here in the Organization. So how did you of all people earn its loyalty?" Sophia asks as she raises her hand causing the Lumber Jack to pause instantly.

"My loyalty has never been in question unlike some around here still I don't know what you're talking about?" Ollie says in a less insane tone as he stares at the ring looking to see if there's any damage from the pummeling the Jack just gave it.

"They first encountered it only miles outside of the cave. A convoy of three trucks surrounding the main transport, you being its precious cargo when they were first attacked. The Beast was relentless attacking at strange times from all angles like it was toying with them.

One by one it picked off the trucks without anyone seeing a thing. Massive claw marks appeared all over on each vehicle before the armored roofs were ripped off and the drivers ripped to pieces. The invisible beasts blood stained mouth appeared only after the third team was gone. That gave the Jacks a sight and they took it, hitting the beast with all they had and finally shaking it off their tail. My glorious Jacks made their heroic stand allowing the transport to escape." Sophia says as she walks over inspecting the small ring before putting it back on.

"But I have a funny feeling that won't be the last time will see the Beast will we? And this time we got a little something for it, unless you have something to say." Sophia assures before getting up and leaving Ollie in the hands of some of the most ruthless agents of the Jacks.

"ON THE GROUND NOW!" is shouted from out of nowhere as the agents bum rush Ollie for being out of the containment square, a piece of tape placed around the floor a foot from the table....

A dark veil sweeps across the horizon as night sets upon the city. Brinly's car slows to a stop diagonally across the street from the offices of Jackson, Wolf, & Associates.

"This is where you think he is?" Brinly asks with an odd expression as she gazes upon her current employers HQ after a very long drive.

"That's the place I've been here once before, it's a terrible place." Archie says as he looks in the rear view mirror still a little unsure of Brinly's answer to his disguise. He feels like a tightly wrapped mummy in a yard sale suit, it's safe to say the fish out of water analogy is hitting the mark at the moment.

"Ok, the best way in is to rip through that door right there." Archie says as he points just past Brinly's nose out the driver side window, "Soon as I do that the clock will be ticking as the alarms will sound and the Jacks will swarm. We can stop everybody after we reach Ollie and the Chronometer."

Brinly tries to interject but is unsuccessful as Archie continues to rattle off his smash and grab plan.

"I'll hold them off while you find Ollie, can you handle that?" Archie finally takes a break from his explanation as he waits for Brinly's response.

Brinly just smiles for the moment trying to act like she had considered what Archie had to say as she opens up her backpack and rummages through it for only a moment or two before pulling out an access badge for the Jackson, Wolf, & Associates building.

"Or we could just sneak in." Brinly says with a chuckle as they take a moment to re-strategize before hopping out of her car and bee lining to the door in question.

"Here goes nothing." Brinly says as the door unlocks allowing them both to enter into this secret society's most treasured sanctuary without tripping a single alarm.

It's quiet inside the building, unusually quiet Brinly notices as she leads Archie along navigating toward the destination Archie described with your every once in a while short cut to avoid being seen by the many Jacks that fill the place.

Brinly finds a long hallway with doors down each side similar to her old high school. She sneaks a peek into a couple of doors as they quickly move through the building.

"This is clergy section of the Jacks society they record everything going on in their perspective view and they have a vast view on the world." Archie explains as they look around in an office before something catches his attention from where they just came from.

The two duck through an office door when sounds of a troop of Jacks echo behind them finding themselves hid out in the office they were just looking at. It's full of desks that circle around a large board covered in old photos and hand written information.

On the top of the board written in big bold letters was the phrase…

'The Bruhaha'

"They make a mean cocktail." Archie says in reference to the centuries old supernatural night club known only as the Bruhaha.

But before Brinly can ask a single question, voices at the door at the back of the office alerts the duo to slip out the exit diagonal to where they entered.

Straight across the hall they rush and through a large set of double doors again staying just out of sight of the Jacks.

Brinly takes a few calming breaths realizing that was a close one and not having a good idea of how she'll react if they're caught, i.e. passing out. If her nerves were getting the better of her she'd never show it.

The room is a vast cathedral of old oil paintings with smaller ones underneath too many to even count as they run to the other side where another set of doors reside.

The large oil paintings are of the most infamous men and women to call themselves Jacks while the smaller paintings below are of their retirees, or in other words, the people they hunted down and brutally eradicated from existence. There's a plaque that resides in front of every painting giving the life history of the Jack including his or her full name and how many kills or retirees they had.

Though one certain oil painting catches Brinly's eye as they near the end causing her to stop and read the plaque below the painting.

"Did you know this?" Brinly asks as she finishes reading about the most well known Jack of them all, "The Ripper was a Jack? Did you know that?"

"Yes he was, but I'm more curious of this Jack right here?" Archie says as Brinly turns to find nothing only the outline of where a large oil painting once hung along with twice as many retirees than the Ripper's.

"Looks like even the Jacks have their dirty little secrets." Brinly says as they get back to searching out their friend inside this fun house for the criminally insane. What's waiting for them on the other side of the doors is the Jacks answer to that particular dirty little secret.

"Both of you stand down and come with Me." the grizzled voice of Carver Grains announces catching Brinly by total surprise as she exits the Jacks hall of fame room.

"Jeez they did a real number on you didn't they big fella?" Archie says as he steps in between this behemoth of a man and Brinly. Archie turns to Brin and assures her, "Go I got this. You worry about finding him."

Upon hearing Archie's boastful comment Carver swings with all his might, no reason on holding back on this guy who thinks he's got this covered. Boy is Carver surprised when Archie catches his punch with the slightest of effort.

"Oh poor giant man you thought I was merely human." Archie chuckles as he snatches Carver off his feet before throwing him through the wall of the Bruhaha office, "You're in for the fight of your life big boy."

And the fight is on as Archie and Carver square off in an epic duel. Each feeling the need to prove they are the stronger specimen.

Carver snatches Archie up by the neck squeezing as tight as he can before slinging him back out of the offices growling to the Jacks pouring in to "CLEAN THAT UP!!!" as he points at the demolished office before stepping out into the hall where Archie waits.

"Impressive, looks like I'll have to stop holding back." Carver says with a smile as he launches another attack more fearsome than the first.

Copious amounts of Jacks round the corner anxious for their chance to contain the Erased, a Deity banished to earth from his existence as a God. It' doesn't matter how hard they try the Jacks alone won't be able to over power the dangerous skeleton man going by the name Archie. Their best bet is to lock him away in a cell designed just for him. …

Now lost in the shuffle from the chaos Archie has got brewing, Brinly makes her way on after taking the stairs up several flights before stepping into an empty hall, she realizes she should've been seen a dozen times or so by now but its like she's invisible or something.

Brin's not complaining mind you, it actually makes it easier to search for more than just Ollie. She's searching for answers to who it is she's been working for?

Brinly gets her answer around the next corner of the seemingly abandoned level of the building.

"Monsters... I work for Monsters." Brinly says with a tear on her cheek as she stands with her eyes locked on to a young child clinging to her mother right in the middle of the holding cells.

The cells on both sides of the long hallway Brinly walked down are filled to the brim with people some were left terribly scarred from the attack that changed them.

The little girl has the greenest eyes Brinly has ever seen, her clothes are tattered and it looks like the two of them have been on 'road rashed' end of a long ride.

"I'm so sorry." Brinly softly says to the little girl who reaches out revealing the horrific scar that branches off down her arm as she flattens her hand on the glass before asking, "Help us?"

The torture this little girl must have endured is truly more than Brinly can stand as she quickly scans for the release lever.

"It's on the wall at the end of the hall." The little girl says as she gestures the direction with her head while never letting loose of her mother.

"I'll help you for a question answered. Favor for a favor." Brinly says as she locates the release lever without taking a step. The little girl nods accepting Brinly's terms.

"Have you seen the Jacks bring in Ollie... The Time Broker?" Brinly asks recognizing that several of the people being held perked up once they heard Ollie's nickname.

"Yes the Broker is in the building, if I were to guess I'd say he's on an interrogation floor. That's all I can tell you." the little girl says as Brinly realizes the legend of the Time Broker spreads far and wide as a slew of Jacks round the corner blocking Brinly's escape, she rushes back to the lever.

"Stop where you are or we'll be forced to shoot!" is shouted from somewhere within the crowd of Jacks better known as the Handlers.

The Handlers are made up of some of the most morally flexible people the Jacks can recruit to do the jobs no one else wants to do.

Namely slaughter countless men, women and children anytime the work order comes through. And that's the thing isn't it because every Jack will fight a werewolf to the death bare handed if necessary.

But when that werewolf turns back to its human form it's a totally different ball game for some Jacks, who fail to see the wolf hiding in plain sight. Those Jacks prefer to capture a person accused of lycanthropy and bring them in as apposed to the kill on sight rule of a wolf.

And that's where the Handlers come into play because man, woman or child it doesn't matter. No wolf is safe from their reach.

"It was enough." is all Brinly says as she raises her hand placing her index finger on the handle at first before quickly wrapping her hand around it.

The Handlers only have the time to throw their hands up in a pleading motion for Brinly to stop before she drops the handle manually opening all the cells on the floor.

The silent alarm sounds alerting all the Handlers here and throughout the building of the impending danger as a secret escape hatch opens right beside Brinly.

The little girl steps out of her cell timidly at first but gaining confidence with each step till she's standing in between the Handlers and her savior.

"Get back in your CELL!" Jacks shout as they approach the little girl in a defensive stance with weapons drawn.

The little girl's reaction is priceless as she simply yawns and stretches her arms out while seamlessly sliding into a bipedal wolf form as easy as spinning around. Her fur turned a golden brown all except for her scar it turned a light blue like a bolt of lightening as it traveled up her arm.

She leans back giving a long howl pausing for only a moment to glance at Brinly with a wink before translating for the unassuming Handlers, "What I said was, kill them, KILLTHEM ALL!"

Brinly doesn't hesitate escaping out the hatch shutting away all the blood curdling screams when she seals the escape hatch shut.

The chaos that ensued on the other side of that steel door will forever become a legendary tale of werewolf revenge passed down from parent to child for the rest of time. …

Chapter Seven

Hiding in Plain Sight

In the Jackson, Wolf, & Associates commons area there's many Jacks just going through their everyday routines like normal. The raging storm of violence brought on by the fury of the recently freed wolves has yet to reach them.

A table full of Jacks at the far end of the room burst into laughter as they one up each others stories of the week's shenanigans.

"Check it out! Look who scored tickets ...ringside." A late arrival to the table says as he plops down nearly spilling his fellow Jacks drinks in the process.

"No way!", "Holy shit those are ringside!", "Who did you have to blow?" is just a few of the comments about the coveted seats to one of the biggest rematches in boxing history.

"Hey who's Jackie decorating for?" the ticket holder asks as he watches a group of Jacks and Jackies rush to finish taping up the streamers and light the candles on the cake.

"It's Jack's last day." A Jack responds as he stares along with his buddy while fantasizing about his own retirement.

"It's always Jack's last day." another agent at the table grunts as he picks up his half eaten tray and leaves the company of his two friends; a moderate annoyance for a less frustrating environment. He gives a slight wave as he heads back to finish up the days work before slipping out early to beat the traffic.

The rest of his friends continue to get the most of their break before clocking back in as they wait on their piece of the cake yet to be cut in celebration of merry ole Jack's last day.

No one in the commons area realizes what's coming for them. The ravenous appetites for vengeance that will only be satisfied by Jacks' blood…

The wolves held their howls in till after they surprised their mortal enemies. The unsuspecting Jacks had their whistles and all the deterrents to stop the average werewolf, buts these aren't your average werewolves. They've endured round the clock torture from the Jacks many deterrents for months some years making them more tolerant to the ear piercing sounds of the infamous silver whistle.

It takes only seconds for the entire commons area to grow deathly silent. The only sound being the soft droplets of blood hitting the floor from the horror movie come to life as all the Jacks lay slaughtered or turning into a blood thirsty beast adding numbers to the pack.

Every new mindless werewolf knows only one thing, to obey their Alpha no questions asked. Those who disobey are made an example of to the rest of the pack. It's a reminder of who's in charge and the little golden wolf cub love to remind them who is in charge as she saunters over and takes a taste before she pushes over merry ole Jack's cake.

"Should've used butter cream!" is all the little Alpha says as she orders the pack onward, spreading throughout the building like a cancerous disease. …

One level down from the wildly ferocious pack of wolves, having the time of his life in the Happy Jacks commons area, Archie is... well let's just say he's in his element.

Archie switches up between retiring (their words) the hoards of the same name dummies to their 'genetic experiment gone wrong' who just doesn't understand the meaning of quit. While joking about those agents being so stupid they had to have the same name.

Carver lands a devastating punch to Archie's invisible abdomen with enough force to crush concrete. The gesture is instantly returned in kind by a left from Archie who apparently hits harder since his punch brought Carver to one knee.

Slowly Archie raises the extinguished behemoth's chin up for the final blow when something in the air catches his attention. It started as a low roar too low for the average human to hear, but Archie heard it and so does Carver.

Like an explosion of raw energy the wolves burst onto the scene, red eyed and ready to rip everyone's throat out as they fill up every inch of the corridor.

Running full stride a wolf leaps out at Carver, missing him and Archie by centimeters as its steel trap of a mouth continues to snap open and closed hoping to snare someone in its jagged teeth as it flips over them.

The wolves become the Jacks main focus as they turn their attention on the enormous numbers surrounding them. The wolves easily out number the Jacks on the corridor three to one leaving Archie to brush off and be on his merry way, until Carver grabs him by the neck.

"Where do you think you're going pip squeak, I ain't through with you yet." Carver growls as he slings Archie through ceiling after ceiling till Archie lands somewhere in the upper levels of the Jackson Wolf & Associates building. …

Two levels below Archie's landing spot, Brinly shuffles through the shadows while looking for the interrogation room housing Ollie. Her list of six rooms has shrunk in half, with the remaining rooms yet to be accounted for are on this floor.

Brinly's noticed the activity in the place has become more excited like a swarm of bees gathering to protect their hive from the bear poking at it since she unleashed the wolves. They've been a true asset in her search for her guy.

Brinly couldn't help falling just a bit for Oliver. Taking her years of fascination on the Chronometer aside she really enjoyed Ollie's company, his stories and just how it felt when she was around him. She missed him and will do everything in her power to see him again.

Quickly Brin freezes in her tracks while a passing Jack and his partner stop in mid sentence and mid step right in front of her.

"Do you smell that? It smells like perfume?" the Jack says before turning to find no one there. Brinly had quietly slid into the vacant office behind her before they could turn around.

As soft as a baby bunny on a felt blanket, Brinly locks the door and crawls behind the desk to wait this out. To be honest she's starting to get use to the routine as she counts down to when the Jacks should leave.

"What have you gotten yourself into now Ms. Blevins?" Brinly says under her breath mimicking her sometimes over protective yet caring mentor Professor Giest. You see she realizes what she's doing is crazy; it's just that she can't help herself.

Calling it 'fatigue' the Jacks continue on their original path ignoring all the signs since it's so close to shift change.

'Just like clockwork' Brinly thinks aloud about the Jacks routine, she's gotten use to ducking for cover to avoid them while on her search, the Jacks are nothing if not predictable.

But just then the phone on the desk Brinly is hiding under starts to ring. Fearing it will gain the attention of the two recently noisy Jacks. Brinly does the only thing she can…

She answers it and gets the surprise of a lifetime.

"Professor? How did you?..." Brinly asks confused at who's on the other end of the line as the Professor takes the conversation over.

"Brinly my dear, listen to me carefully. You're so close now. You're on the same floor as the Chronometer. Find him, find him and I'll find you." The Professor says and then he whispers something into the phone in a language rarely heard by the human ear.

The effect is instant as Brinly's end of the line goes dead.

"See you soon."...

Elsewhere in the building that is slowly collapsing into chaos, agents' secure their chief in an act of protection from the wolves and something else in the shadows.

"Mam! The wolves have been released!" an agent says as he barges in to the interrogation room where Ollie is being held.

"Which ones?" Sophia asks as she takes her gaze off of years of torment nicknamed the Time Broker.

"All of them! They've already over run the Handlers and are now rampaging throughout the building. They're headed this way." The agent says as he urges her to seek safety.

"Where's Carver?" Sophia asks without the slightest hint of worry in her tone, having a thousand plus years to lean back on takes the worry out of most things.

"In an all out war with the Erased, we need to leave Mam." The agent responds while continuing to follow protocol and help his leader to safety.

"Bring Carver back." is all Sophia says as she stands over Ollie with an evil gleam in her eye before adding, "Let's go big boy, it seems you've had quite the fan club show up here. I think its time we take a little trip to an inaccessible place. Did you pack a coat?"

Sophia waves her Jacks to release the Time Broker from his chair while continuing to keep his hands cuffed.

"You sure you want to do this without your heavy hitter? Maybe we should wait on him, so where did you send Paul Bunyan anyways? I kind of miss him." Ollie says with a chuckle as he's forced to his feet and ordered to walk at gun point into a horror show like none they've ever barely seen.

"If I were you I would be less worried about the whereabouts of Carver Grains and be more worried about where you're fixing to spend the next thousand years." Sophia says as she leads Ollie and a small goon squad of Jacks to a hidden passage behind a painting of her father just as the alarms trip alerting Sophia's agents that something just landed on this floor.

"You two go see what tripped the alarm and you stay close to the Broker." Sophia orders her three Jack goon squad to split up. She keeps one Jack with her to force Ollie down the dark corridor behind the painting while leaving the other two Jacks to their fate.

They were only halfway to the other end of the corridor when the Jack hears it, something in the shadows. He opens fire and the bursts of light given off by the rifle only shows a glimpse of what's waiting for them at the other end of the passage.

"RETREAT! RETREAT! We've got a breach!" the Jack yells just before he's snatched away returning the dead silence and pitch black to the passage.

"I smell the Broker in here?" comes from the darkness as the unlikely duo decides its best to not argue as they swiftly put it in reverse.

"Broker your girlfriend is somewhere in this building, here to save you." the voice calls out again as they near the exit from where they first entered the passage, though the comment slows Sophia's pace as she's now curious to what the wolf is talking about.

"She's the one who freed us, give her our thanks." The voice growls ending with a chomp so close to Ollie's ear he lunges back falling out through the painting that hid the entrance to the secret passage where they began.

"Careful she's a wild one." is the last thing whispered out of the passage, it seems the wolves choose not to follow Ollie and Sophia through as if there was something else on that floor worse than revenge filled werewolves.

"Look if you plan on getting out of here in one piece we're going to have to work together." Ollie says with a reluctant tone and a look of regret as soon as the words exit his lips.

"Oh yeah I bet you think I would just fall for the 'you and me team' just like the good old days? Please… Keep your mouth shut and your head down unless you plan on losing it!" Sophia shouts as her more tenacious attitude takes over forcing her pistol deep into Ollie's back before she gruffly says, "Move!" …

In the upper levels of the building Carver and the Erased continue to wreck shop as they fight with all their might trying to force the other to yield. Carver is surprised by the strength of the Erased. This is the first time that Carver has met anyone close to his power level. But that doesn't matter now, because this battle is at its destination.

Carver has fought tooth and nail, literally, to lead Archie to this point. Just over Archie's shoulder hid behind a set of unassuming double doors there's a special cell designed to hold beings of great strength. And that's exactly where Carver plans to put the Erased.

Suddenly a distress signal from somewhere on Carver goes off alerting him that Sophia is in trouble. In an instant Carver lashes out at Archie grabbing his foe by the throat before slinging him like a fastball over home plate into the cell.

Archie slams the wall with the force of a bomb. His impact sent an earth quaking jolt of energy throughout the building while causing the cell to erupt to life as lights and alarms go off.

"It's over. You're...Over." Carver vaguely says as he turns to save Sophia.

Archie takes a step and both the floor and ceiling begin to close causing Archie to take heed.

"I wouldn't do that if I were you. You take one more step and the industrial hydraulic presses placed above and below you will trigger, erasing the Erased. You get my drift?" Carver asks as he leaves the Erased trapped leaping into action to find Sophia. …

Back on Sophia's floor Carver arrives just in the nick of time as he breaks through the ceiling to take the brunt of an attack meant for Sophia from the invisible monster he first met back in the desert.

Shielded by Carver, Sophia gets the chance she needed to push Ollie back into an interrogation room sealing it shut before racing off to the armory for gun with a bit more fire power.

"Hold it off Carver, I'll be right back." is the last thing Carver hears as the monster rips into him with its razor sharp teeth.

"I WOULD HURRY IF I WERE YOU!" is all Carver shouts back as he gets his grip on the beast allowing him to throw it off balance as he swings behind it putting it in a choke hold.

Carver's unbreakable grip is legendary and now that it's around the beast it won't be able to escape. Problem with that is now Carver can't escape either and he's pissed the beast off. …

Outside the building of Jackson, Wolf, & Associates it's your average Chicago night as the younger crowd still prowls the streets looking for a good time. None of the locals have a clue to the war being waged inside.

That's about to change…

Wolves burst out of the building from all sides once they've found the exit, revenge is sweet and Jacks blood deserves to be spilled, but freedom is sweeter. "Another time!" the wolves all howl as they take their first breaths of fresh air in months for some of them.

The reaction from the nearby crowd of people just out on the town is evolving from excitement to concern to horror. Finally ending in sheer panic as they scatter for their lives, some are faster than others.

Within seconds of the first wave of escapees, the Jacks security protocols kick in sealing off the entire building from the outside world while sending enough Jacks out to round up the strays. …

Back inside Brinly seems to appear in front of the solid steel door holding a set of keys. She thumbs through the set for only a moment or two before finding the right one, "Bingo."

The large steel door swings open to find Ollie passed out in the chair at the desk.

“Ollie oh my God wake up, wake up!” Brinly frantically says as she shakes then slaps him trying to wake Ollie up.

“I am awake. My eyes are swollen shut, please stop slapping me.” Ollie says with an assertive yet gentle tone.

“Listen we have to get out of here. I think that monster you saw at the Guise house is here and I set the wolves free, I’m not so sure that was a good idea now. Anyways we got to go!” Brinly says as she flips through the keys till she finds the one for Ollie’s cuffs.

“We can’t leave till I get this off and collect what’s mine. It’s hanging around the boss’s neck.” Ollie adds as Brinly un-cuffs him.

“Ollie there’s no place to put a key in this thing around your wrist?” Brinly says as she inspects the device encasing the Chronometer.

“It doesn’t unlock.” Ollie unfortunately says after Sophia assured him he’ll never get that off during her torturous interrogation.

“What are we going to do?” Brin says as Ollie reaches for her to help him up.

“Well I’ll tell you one thing. We’re not going to stick around here.” Ollie says with a wincing chuckle as they waddle their way out before the monster or Sophia shows up in here.

“You know Archie’s here, somewhere?” Brinly says as she helps Ollie get his stride back. The beating he took at the hands of the Jacks has left its mark.

“Perfect let’s find him.” Ollie says figuring Archie’s unbridled strength should be enough to tear the bracelet off the Chronometer giving him his access to his time again. After that they can get the key from Sophia destroy Corvan and escape this madhouse without detection before it crumbles to the ground.

"Easy peezy." Ollie thinks aloud drawing a curious look from Brinly as they stumble upon the hole in the floor made by their currently missing boney friend.

"Ok, maybe not?" Ollie chirps back at his last comment as he slowly leans over looking down the hole just to see if he can spot Archie only to find werewolves running rampant everywhere but the floor they're on.

"That's odd?"...

Downstairs in the main lobby the few fortunate Jacks begin to reenter the premises soaked in the blood of their enemies while the less fortunate lay in the streets outside bleeding out at the feet of the ravenous werewolves who hunger for more.

"Head count, how many are missing?" the Jacks squad leader asks as he gets a quick count; it isn't good. If they don't get a handle on this soon they may not survive the night.

"Twenty two missing, fifteen dead, twelve of them started to change or else it would've only been three dead." Jack's second in command announces as he catches a glimpse of a stranger in the lobby causing him to leap into action.

"ON THE FLOOR NOW!!! Who are you!!" the second shouts from behind the barrel of his drawn weapon as he slowly creeps up on the mystery man.

The rest of the Jacks respond in kind as they jump into motion surrounding the stranger from all sides with their weapons drew causing the unwelcome man to slowly raise his hands as he looks up at the leader with an unusual look on his face.

Upstairs at that very moment Brinly notices the stranger on a security screen they just passed and stops in her tracks.

"Professor?" Brinly says as she turns back to stare at the screen in the vacant security post.

"Brin?" Ollie says as he feels uneasy staying in one place for too long, like sitting ducks.

"Ollie I know him, we have to help." Brinly frantically responds as she pulls Ollie toward the elevator they were headed to even faster than before.

"I don't know how much help I will be without my Chronometer, but OK." Ollie says with a friendly nudge as he sees Sophia round the corner with a gun bigger than her as the elevator doors close.

BOOM!!!

An explosion rips through the doors severing one of the cables of the descending elevator sending Ollie and Brin on the ride of their life.

"Gotcha!" Sophia satisfyingly says as she listens to the elevator drop while the smoke still roles out of the barrel of her weapon.

Chapter Eight

A Deal's a Deal

In the main lobby the sound of an elevator pummeling to the ground takes precedence over the lone mystery man as he answers the question shouted at him only moments earlier.

"Who am I? Who am I? Well, I guess if you ever needed a definition to the term God... I am it." the mystery man announces causing everyone to freeze in their tracks with merely a thought.

"I'm here for the Chronometer and only the Chronometer. Those that appose me will perish. All others go free." The man plainly says like he's not outnumbered as a sea of Jacks heed the call to arms funneling into the main lobby. ...

Inside said elevator plummeting to their doom Ollie frantically slams his protected Chronometer against the panel trying to get any kind of result out of the elevator besides death.

Amazingly Ollie hits the right button engaging the emergency brakes on the runaway death trap and miraculously they begin to slow finally stopping completely.

"Where are we?" Brinly asks as she clamors up off the elevator floor.

"I'm not sure, are you ok?" Ollie asks as he's in the process of picking himself up as well.

Leaping up Ollie knocks the cover off the emergency exit grabbing the side of the roof to keep him from dropping. His feet dangle there for only a moment or two while he takes a breath then finally he pulls himself through the hatch. Ollie won't deny that things are bit more of a task without the help of his trusty Chronometer but there's no stopping him now.

"Let's go, up and out." Ollie says as he reaches in for Brin pulling her up into the darkness of the elevator shaft.

"Looks like we're stuck somewhere in between the third and second floors I think I can get the doors to open but we'll still have to fight our way down to your friend without any weapons." Ollie reminds her with a jingle of his wrist and a wince in pain from the action. Once he unlocks the Chronometer he'll gain access to his time again, allowing Ollie to rapidly heal from his ordeal.

"I won't stop, let's go!" Brinly retorts as she stands on one side of the doors mimicking Ollie's movements by grabbing the manual release handle and pulling up.

THE THIRD FLOOR…

Stepping up and through the wide enough crack in the third floor doors first thing they notice is how quiet it is. It looks like an abandoned battle ground as lights flicker in the distance walls knocked down and a strange smell in the air. Jacks are scattered throughout the hallways along with a winding river of blood proof the wolves have come and gone on this floor.

Without a second thought Brinly eyes the stairway door and off they go, rushing across the hall just in case a wolf lingers in the shadows. Brinly bursts through the door to the stairwell like an explosion without even slowing down to take notice that they're not alone.

Ollie catches her shoving her through the steel door of the second floor just as a two man kill squad of Jacks rounded the steps headed to the top floor.

THE SECOND FLOOR …

"Holy shit!" is all Ollie can muster as he has to bare witness to what is currently happening in the warzone known as the second floor. And for lack of better words its torturous agony as wolves slip through the shadows devouring every Jack they see. It's looking more and more like the floor above it as the fighting goes on.

This is the first time Ollie's ever seen the Jacks out numbered and getting the other end of the whooping stick. Brinly stares at all the bodies with the truest of regret knowing it was her that released this nightmare.

'DING-DING'…

They both hear it over all screams and gun shots as the doors at the other end of the hallway spring open and Sophia steps out in what looks like slow motion as she scans for the duo.

"RUN!" as he grabs Brinly's hand before darting off within the chaos adding, "There's another way, come on!"

The two disappear around a corner as Sophia opens fire dropping wolves and Jacks alike just to make a pathway. Sophia grins at the challenge it's been years since she's been on a hunt. And her tracking skills are just one of her many talents that made her a legend.

THE FIRST FLOOR...

Neither Brinly nor Ollie even took the time to look at the condition of the second floor. Forgoing the assured insanity inside for the rescue Brinly so desperately wants to perform.

THE GROUND FLOOR...

They made it is the glorious feeling Brinly feels as she rushes out to find her mentor and longtime friend. Ollie has already accepted what they will see. He knows it took too long to get down here he just hasn't had the heart to tell Brin. He figures at best they'll find the Professor's body riddled with lead and at worst just his bones. But what they found was nothing like what they had prepared for.

"MOTHERFUCKER!" Ollie furiously shouts as he jumps in between the Professor and Brinly in an attempt to protect her from his longest living nightmare.

What they see is nearly beyond description. As they gaze out into the middle of this floor of floating Jacks each Jack frozen in place like a statue as gravity seems to forgotten they were there.

"Hello Oliver, it's been awhile... my, my, look at your precious time piece all wrapped up and just out of reach. What a shame." The Professor says with an evil gleam in his eyes.

"What's wrong Ollie? And how are you doing that Professor you never told me you had powers?!" Brinly says with a touch of soreness in her tone about the secret the Professor kept from her, it only gets worse from here.

"He ain't your Professor Brin, that's Corvan Sin." Ollie says as he eases Brinly back the way they came now wishing they had went and found Archie first.

"Actually, I am her Professor and a bit more if I'm being completely honest with myself." Corvan announces as reveals his true form while moving out of the center of the floating Jacks making his way toward the duo with some residual Jacks following Corvan's magnetic pull.

"I think I'll snatch a period from you this time." Ollie confidently says giving reference to a period of time in the millions of years such as the Jurassic Period only realizing afterwards that he can't.

"Run!" Ollie shouts as they both turn to seek shelter.

Corvan freezes them both with a thought then drags Oliver to his hand before slinging Ollie across the lobby and into a stone pillar again with only a thought.

BOOM!!!

Out of nowhere Corvan is hit with a blast of energy so strong it shoots the deity through the mass of Jacks who all drop out of the air like gravity was just switched back on. Corvan hits the ground hard showing no signs of life, for the moment as the energy dances across him like a spider web made of lighting.

“Hands off the merchandise pal.” Sophia shouts as she enters the lobby holding the smoking gun that’s killed a God. Sophia’s first thought is to check on Ollie, it infuriates her that even after all this time there’s still a spot in her heart for the Time Broker.

The dwindling Jacks forces fill up the lobby ready to lay down their lives to protect Sophia. Quickly they begin reviving the few Jacks on the ground who are still clinging to life while others begin to pick up the dead deity’s body.

With a wink of the eye, the very first motion Corvan could muster after the blast from Sophia’s gun, every Jack in his distant view dropped dead on the spot.

“He's not dead!” a Jack yells seeing what just happened to all his fellow Jacks while standing just out of the view of the non responsive deity.

Sophia takes cover behind a pile of rubble from the partially collapsed first floor along with a handful of her Jacks that survived who scramble to do the same before the deity who’s slowly starting to move again sees them too.

At the same moment Ollie wakes up with a fresh gash on his forehead. His first thought is of Brinly but its Sophia that catches his attention as she’s quietly waving him over to her under the safety of cover from the deity’s gaze.

“What happened?” Ollie asks as he tries to get his bearings back. Sophia wipes her lost loves face off the best she can before slapping him then kissing him. The slap was for the thousand year gift Ollie bestowed on her, the kiss was long overdue.

"Listen to me Ollie before it breaks free, you make my fucking blood boil to no ends and we got a lot to atone for but if we both want to survive tonight, we'll have to do it together. So let's make a deal?" Sophia says as she pulls out the key to the Chronometer handing it to Ollie without even saying what she desires in return.

"A deal, huh?" Ollie says doubting that Sophia can keep her word but she did just hand him the key to stopping Corvan. And by judging the looks of the place they all will be lucky to see another day if Ollie doesn't do something soon. Of coarse Ollie can't save the day if he can't gain access to the Chronometer.

"Any ideas?" Ollie asks about the device Sophia had clamped around his wrist denying him the access he so desperately desires.

Sophia shrugs before shooting her best guess, "Maybe some immense pressure? That might do the trick, maybe?"

"Great, immense pressure, guess I'll see what I can find. You wouldn't be at liberty to tell me where Archie is would you?" Ollie says with a roll of his eyes at Sophia's inadequate response before leaping into action to get Brinly who is laying on the ground out cold.

"Brin, we got to get out of here, wake up, wake up... WAKE UP." Ollie says as he works to revive her. The first thing he sees is the tears that roll down Brinly's terrified face as she reaches up to Ollie.

"Ollie I'm sacred! Something's wrong, with me, he did something to me, said something to me." Brinly says with the look of a shattered soul that's just learned the truth.

“It’s ok, we’ll get you out of here. I’ve got the key now, I just have to get this clamp off and we’re home free.” Ollie assures her as he helps Brin back to her feet unsure of how exactly he’s going to do that before Corvan revives himself and levels the building.

But their time has just run out as Brinly gets re-stuck in her tracks by a monster pretending to be her mentor who just broke free and now holds her fate in his hands.

“Well, well, well, who do we have here? If it isn’t my favorite protégé Ms. Brinly Rachel Blevins, My child, I think it’s time for the truth about what you really are.” Corvan says as he leans up against Brinly with no fear of Ollie or his Chronometer makes Corvan relish the moment even more.

Ollie lunges at Corvan trying to free Brin but is met with the cold sinking feeling in his spine that’s keeping him from twitching so much as a pinky, put there by the deity.

“There that should hold you, now where was I? Oh yes Brinly’s true lineage. You may think that your dear ole dad is your father, and yes he was a good man but you’re not his daughter.” Corvan says as he waltz around the two of them watching as Brinly’s eyes are locked onto Ollie’s each having a piercing look of hopelessness at each other.

“Carolynn Rachel Blevins, Your Mother, she was an amazing woman Brinly. Your Mother came from a long lost line of descendents loyal to the Guise. And even though she was lost to the people, Carolynn stayed connected to me." Corvan says as he leisurely walks around the lobby slightly waving his hands causing all the debris and remnants of the werewolf ravaged building to be brushed aside clearing a path like magic.

"Carolynn had been happily married to her sweetheart wanting nothing more than a child to call her own. She'd tried everything from the promised to work 'just sign here' methods of procreation to the doctor's less credible than that with her husband Harold holding her hand every step of the way, still no child to call her own. I watched her pray to me every night and every day to give her what she desired most of all. After everything else failed her Carolynn went on undeterred without missing a single day of prayer.

So one night no more special than any of the others in her long and tragic life I choose to answer her prayers. I visited in the night choosing Harold Bailey Blevins as my image while the real Harold worked in his office down stairs. Don't worry I serviced him too as your Mother, I didn't have to but it just seemed right." Corvan says with a chuckle and even a bigger grin when he sees how Ollie is taking it; torturing the Pendulums is like mother's milk to Corvan.

"Nine months to the day, MY beautiful bundle of joy took her first breaths in this world. I knew she would be amazing so I choose to hide in plain sight so to speak just to keep a watchful eye on her." Corvan laughs in a hauntingly creepy manor as he releases both Ollie and Brin from his paralyzing grasp while he takes a break to let what he's said sink in.

Brinly drops to her knees looking up to the sky while pleading, "No, no, no, no, please no." she can feel it in her bones, he's telling the truth.

"I'm afraid so my dear but it's not all stale cookies and soured milk." is all Corvan says as he brushes his hand over Brinly's face causing her eyes to close while Corvan unlocks the closed connection inside of Brinly.

Suddenly she blurts out, "I'm sorry Ollie! I'm so, so sorry!" causing Ollie to shout at Corvan to stop as he swings his shielded Chronometer with all his might hitting the deity in the back of the head hard enough to crack the average man's head wide open.

Unfazed at Ollie's feeble attempt to crush his skull, Corvan longingly looks at his daughter before responding with a terrible grin.

"No. She can't un-see what she's been shown. Look at her the realization of what she is... What she REALLY is. I've unlocked her mind guided her way... Look she's at the last door now. Uh oh she's walking through. I'd stand back if I were you." Corvan says boasting as he rambles on making less sense the more he speaks.

That all changes as soon as Brinly's body twists in pain letting out a primal scream from deep with in. "Ollie get out of here, leave me now before it's too late." Brinly begs him as she feels her body begin to warp out of her natural shell. She knows now why she always dreamed of a monster saving her when she was in real trouble, she knows why it never chose to turn on her, she is the monster. Brin's size begins to alter as does her shape. Claws replace her hands and feet while serrated steel teeth now adorn her mouth.

"I'll never leave your side." Ollie strongly states while watching as Brinly becomes the massive monster he barely saw back at the incident on Cypress Lane where he first met Brinly.

"Can you see it now Time Broker? The love of your life is my daughter, the monster you fear lives inside of her. Give me the device and I'll let you go free." Corvan laughs as he waves for his pet to attack Oliver. The monster roars while eyeing Ollie with a look of hunger in her eyes.

All Ollie can do is watch as the monster creeps closer to him with a low growl emanating from within. As much as he would like to run he can't, Corvan made sure of that simply by paralyzing Ollie's movements from the waist down.

But like a man born under a lucky star Ollie's rescue comes in from out of no where in the form of a large squadron of the last active Jacks in the building bursting through the door with guns blazing firing their aim is straight at the three of them, two Jacks wield the same energy weapons Sophia had.

The blasts from those two guns send Corvan for cover and Brinly into action leaving Ollie stuck in the line of fire. She streaks across the lobby in the blink of an eye. Her movements being much faster now in her new Chimera form and boy is she lethal. Disappearing gives the advantage back to her and she makes the very most of it.

Blood explodes out of the Jacks like they each swallowed a bomb. But in actuality their blood loss comes from the invisible teeth of the Chimera as she sinks them deep into her aggressors.

Ollie realizes he should be frightened to a near panic state at this point. Having no way to access his Chronometer and watching the world crumble around him by gun fire, but he's not. In fact he's quite the opposite as he enjoys watching her work.

I mean if it wasn't for the Jacks, Ollie and Brin wouldn't be in this position in the first place. Ollie would still have the protection of his Chronometer keeping all the trouble at bay. Brinly wouldn't be a monster ripping them to pieces, and Archie well we don't know what happened to Archie but he wouldn't have to be waging war in this building if not for the Jacks.

"No that's not right?" Ollie thinks out loud as he realizes who's really to blame. The source of all his pain and of all his horrors isn't the Jacks, though they rank second on his list of evil people they're not the top. That honor goes entirely to Corvan Sin 'The Guise'.

"That's enough." Corvan states calling off the monster as he emerges from his hiding spot where those weapons couldn't reach him.

Quickly the Chimera returns to Corvan's side drenched in blood while purring in a deep rumble and caressing her Father much like a house cat would its food giver.

"Now finish him for me my pet, my love, my protector." Corvan says and with every word the Chimera's growl grows. She leaps out in between her Father and Ollie in a defensive stance showing her razor sharp teeth and unsheathing her dinosaur killing claws.

"Yeah you would force her to do that with me stuck here and her not knowing what she's doing, some god." Ollie prods gaining the exact reaching he wanted as Corvan chuckles for only a moment before releasing his hold on the Time Broker.

"Oh I assure you Brinly is right below the surface watching everything unfold with her own two eyes. There's nothing blocking her from her more savage side anymore. See if you can reach her before she does you." Corvan says with a whistle sending the Chimera into action as Brinly slowly stalks Ollie like a wounded animal whose time is up.

Ollie stumbles back a few steps but only finding it draws the Chimera closer and at a faster pace. So he stops in his tracks and waits for her, she's so primal now, ferocious with every calculated step. It's hard to believe Brinly is in there somewhere but there's no other choice but to try and reach her.

"Brinly, I know you're in there. I know you can see me, stop what you're doing. He's controlling you, fight it. Remember me. You can control this." Ollie says as the Chimera now stands nose to nose with him.

She takes slow breaths exhaling the stench of death all over Ollie as he just stands there with his arms out in an unaggressive manor. She turns her head barely missing Ollie's face with her horn before catching Ollie's eye and at that moment he sees her.

“Hello Brin, well would you just look at the two of us now.” Ollie says in a comforting tone as he reaches up petting Brinly under her chin.

“I'm growing impatient my pet!” Corvan growls causing a jolt of pain to be sent through Brinly’s Chimera form, she roars in agony before staring at Corvan with a long growl.

A single tear rolls down Brinly’s cheek disappearing into her fur before she snaps hold of Ollie’s left arm just as Corvan instructs. It’s over in the blink of an eye and suddenly everything is moving in slow motion for Ollie who hasn’t had the heart to look down to see where exactly she took his arm off at, was just above the wrist or did she go all the way to the elbow.

It’s Corvan’s shouts of disapproval that causes Ollie to look down to see what she took.

“Immense force.” is all Ollie can muster as he stares at the Chronometer for what feels like the first time since he initially adorned the watch.

Brinly roars out at Corvan as she now stands protecting Ollie as he spins the dials releasing enough time for him to heal completely in only a second.

Corvan lashes out trying to get to the Chronometer as fast as he can but is met by the full force of Brinly’s strength. Brin sinks her teeth deep into Corvan’s neck dragging him across the lobby before taking a blast of energy from the deity causing her to be thrown back and out of the path to Ollie. But that doesn’t matter now.

Suddenly an explosion of energy bursts out of the Chronometer…

AND TIME STANDS STILL.

Brinly is stopped in the air just before she hit the wall. Corvan is stuck to the floor unable to move a muscle. All the Jacks are stuck in place, but to be honest their all mostly dead at this point, so no real wow moment there. And lastly the wolves, on every floor are frozen in time.

The only person able to move at this moment is reveling in the fact at how the tables have finally turned now as Ollie walks over to Corvan while tinkering with the Chronometer on his wrist. Ollie shows off the Chronometer to his foe and it's the last dial added to it that gains Corvan's attention. It's the last thing the deity will see.

"Corvan Sin, The Guise, it saddens me to inform you that today is the last day of your life. I hope you found solace in the eons of life you enjoyed..." Ollie announces reminiscent of an old gospel preacher with the giggles before pausing…

"This is for my Parents." Ollie whispers to himself before twisting the new dial and hitting the button…

A flash of energy like none Ollie's ever seen, bursts out of the Chronometer encapsulating Corvan's body. Instantly the deity is drained of his outer layers revealing so much of the power underneath.

Corvan fights with all the power he has left but with every second that passes the deity losses ground and slowly he is peeled like an onion till only the bones remain. If you think Ollie stopped there you would be wrong. He didn't stop till there was nothing left.

And just like that a Deity had been wiped off the face of the earth…

Everything is still now.

"It's nice." Ollie thinks aloud as he admires the calmness of the frozen moment in time he'd never really realized how lucky he was to get to do what he's done for so many years. This gift always came with the wrath of a God that sat like a weight on his shoulders, a weight that is now lifted, vanished from the face of the earth.

It's strange though as Ollie glances around like he's seeing the world through a new set of eyes from the power now coursing through him.

Locating Brinly, Ollie releases her from her frozen state. The Chimera drops to the ground naturally landing on its feet. Brinly looks at Ollie through the Chimera's haunting gaze for only a moment before sliding back into her human form minus her clothes, which is the problem for anyone who instantly grows very large.

Grabbing a blanket and covering her, Ollie starts to ask but is interrupted by Brin. "Are yo..."

"Where is he?! Is he really gone?" Brinly frantically asks as she drops to her knees in disbelief of what all she remembers, which is everything. Everything from the days events all the way back to the first time she remembered dreaming about the monster that would save her when she was in trouble.

"They were never dreams." Brinly softly says as she tries to mentally unpack all the truth that was just handed to her on a golden platter.

"I'm a monster." Brinly now says with her eyes glaring with rage.

"You're not a monster, you're amazing... and you're naked." Ollie says as he hugs her so tight, "I thought I lost you girl."

"I don't understand, you've seen the monster in me. Why are you not scared?" Brinly asks with tears replacing the rage in her eyes.

"Again you're not a monster. A monster wouldn't save her friend. Thanks to you and your ability to shape shift into a giant Chimera I was able to install the key and absorb Corvan completely without draining the time out of anybody else. Guess there's some new functions I got to get use to." Ollie says as he's acknowledges that there's something different about the Chronometer's newest set of ability's unlocked by the key.

"That makes two of us." Brinly says finally showing Ollie that signature smile of hers. Ollie wipes away the last of her tears while helping her up to her feet.

"Come on let's go find you some duds and locate our boney friend. Archie's got to be around here somewhere?" Ollie says as he and Brinly escape out of the room full of Jacks including Sophia Sinclair-Renault still frozen in time. …

Sophia comes back to the here and now much like flipping a switch on. The rest of the Jacks still breathing begin to show subtle signs of movement as well.

It's an agonizing task trying to move for one reason alone, all your muscles instantly cramp after long exposures to time manipulation. That's Sophia's first clue that they've been here for a much longer time than it feels like, it felt like a blink of an eye. Whatever happened while the rest of the surviving Jacks were incapacitated is all over now.

"First priority is to find the Time Broker!" Sophia roars into the radio set to every channel waiting impatiently as she continues to regain motor function in the rest of her limbs. She notices, it doesn't hurt to blink now and is so thankful having never felt an agony quite like it.

"First priority is to find the Time Broker! Respond! Jacks respond!" Sophia shouts again into the silent radio.

"Jacks respond!" Sophia yells one last time before dropping the radio to her side as she lays back to rest. The last thing Sophia remembers is hearing the sound of people in the distance breaching the lobby doors as she passes out. …

Three nights later just as the moon glows bright in the sky casting the shadow of the clock tower over the courtyard near a very well known University in Massachusetts the single shadow of Ollie gets lost in the shade of the tower itself.

Inside the building it's not long before there's a knock on a door. The time is way past that of a doctor being at their office. But this particular doctor doesn't ever seem to leave his work. You can always find Dr. Samuel Chase at the labs no matter the time of day or night.

Ollie knocks again and again before he finally hears rumblings coming from behind the door.

"WHAT IS IT? You're interrupting some very important research! Wasting my valuable time!" this young doctor shouts out from the crack in the opened door yet to raise his welding goggles to actually see who is there.

"Samuel I believe you owe me a debt and since we're talking about time and how valuable it is. I'd say it's time to get square." Ollie states causing the erratic attitude of the young doctor to flip into that of a jovial host as he opens the door inviting Ollie in.

"Hello Broker, wow you haven't aged a day? How may I be of service to you?" Dr. Chase asks getting the surprise of his life the moment he answered the door.

"Grab a jacket and come with me. You wouldn't happen to have a set thermal vision binoculars would you?" Ollie asks stopping a foot from the door for Dr. Chase's response.

"Yeah we have a set, why?" Dr. Chase asks with a bubbling curiosity at what he's about to discover. He always gets this feeling just before a huge discovery.

"Grab them too." Ollie says as he heads out the door like time was of the essence.

So naturally Dr. Chase snatches up the binoculars and leaps toward the door to catch up with the Time Broker asking, "Where are we headed?"

"Outside." is all Ollie says as the two of them disappear from time reappearing out by a tree so fast it looked like they teleported. For the record both Ollie and the doctor had to walk every step to that spot by the tree.

The nighttime air is chili as Ollie stares out into the darkness. "You were correct it is a cool night tonight. Well now that I'm here, why am I here?" Dr. Chase asks as he puts the binoculars up to his eyes scanning the area just because why else bring them out.

"To repay your debt. I got a good friend who needs some help blending back in with the world. You were the first person I thought of so here we are." Ollie announces as he sends out a high pitch whistle drawing out the promise he intends to keep.

Ollie sees Archie's eyes glowing in the opposite direction and adjusts the young doctor's view. The doctor scans for only a moment before he spots his prize.

"Hey, there's a man walking this way? Is that your friend?" Dr. Chase says as he looks up from the thermal image and gets weak in the knees as he sees a skeleton approaching instead of the man in the image.

"That's him." Ollie smiles as he notices Dr. Chase's excitement of the challenge.

"So he's got a body right? We just can't see it? I think I have just the thing for him. How durable is he?" Dr. Chase asks as he stares at the skeleton periodically peering through the binoculars to make sure he's seeing what he thinks he's seeing.

"Very, and call him Archie. He seems to like that." Ollie says just before Archie steps into an ear shot of their conversation.

"A deals a deal and if there's any way to find a bit of normal again I assure you it's with the help of my good friend here, Dr. Samuel Chase. Sam it is my honor to introduce you to my great friend Archie." Ollie says as Sam can't help but to gaze at the skeleton standing before him.

"HELLO. MY NAME IS SAM." Dr. Chase says like he's talking to a small child, Archie's response was priceless.

"What the fuck is wrong with him? Are you sure he's a Doctor?" Archie rattles off about how he's being talked to like a child and catches Dr. Chase off guard once again.

"Trust me Arch, he's got it where it counts." Ollie says with a chuckle as he shakes Archie's gloved hand before waving good bye and disappearing from sight.

"Hey wait a minute?" Archie shouts as he rushes up to ask Ollie one more thing.

"Where are you and the kitten going? In case I need to know where to find you? I may want to show off my new self." Archie says under his breath still not quite trusting the new doctor Ollie introduced him to.

"She's got a craving for adventure, so we're going to start in the jungle of South America. I'll keep an eye out for you." Ollie says with a smile while whispering something meant only for Archie's ears before disappearing again, this time for good. …

Across the quad a mile from where he left Archie with the man planning on giving him a new skin Ollie reappears. He's been very cautious since the escape staying mostly to the shadows. They're still in danger from the Jacks who'll do everything in their power to get to Brinly after realizing she was the monster they were looking for the whole time. That's all they wanted when they had Ollie held prisoner and he knows they won't stop until they have her in a cage.

That's the reason Ollie and Brinly chose to split up on the second day with the plan to meet up at a certain time and place after Ollie makes good on his end of the deal with Archie.

Ollie was meticulous about the details reminding Brinly to stay out of sight and close to her ferocious feline side in case she's spotted by the Jacks.

"They're everywhere, so please be careful and follow the plan." Ollie reminds one more time before giving her a soft kiss on the lips.

All that planning was for not though. …

"Ollie?" Sammy calls out from the shadows of the alley gaining the Time Broker's full attention.

"Sammy? What happened where have you been? I thought you were dead! I haven't seen you since the night you gave me my pages back?" Ollie says as he follows the sound one step too far into the darkness.

Sammy appears right in front of Ollie with tears in her eyes. "Thank god you're ok." Ollie says as he hugs her letting his guard down. And that's when they struck!

BOOM!!! BOOM!!!

Two blasts ring out from beside Sammy lighting both her and Ollie up. The two drop to the ground, Sammy's dead carcass smolders from the electrocution while Ollie's still frozen in place unable to reach his Chronometer and unable to die from the power of the deity that now courses through his veins.

"Time's up, Lover. You should've never asked for help from a Jack, they can't help but to betray you." Sophia says as she nudges the cooked body of her own agent Sammy who served her purpose well while she steps over the frozen body of her one time love of her life.

"Bet you're starting to regret the thousand year gift you bestowed upon me, am I right?" Sophia says as she orders her Jacks to place the Time Broker in a six foot long box made out of the ore found at cave of the Erased after strapping his arms to his side and his feet together.

"Actually it wasn't a thousand year gift. You must've misheard me when I spoke, its a thousand generation gift." Ollie says as he's looks at Sophia from up out of his specially made coffin waiting for it to sink in.

"What are you saying? How long is a generation?" Sophia asks with a confused and growing look of concern on her face.

"Who could really say how long a generation is?" Ollie responds vaguely as he seems to still poke the bear even up to the very end.

"You! You could say how long it is!" Sophia shouts while giving Ollie a searing look for what he's done, cursing her to out live all her kids grand kids, and so on for a thousand generations.

"Well I think if going by the official definition, a generation is a measurement in time with the duration being around twenty to twenty five years, though I'd figure yours to be in the sixty to ninety five year range, if I were you." Ollie says with a satisfying smile having reveled just how much time he really gave Sophia in exchange for the key.

In a fit of emotion Sophia kicks the box initiating the Jacks to seal it shut. Sophia halts the process of covering the coffin locking Ollie in, to take a breath before asking one last question, "Where is the girl?"

Ollie just chuckles at the comment causing Sophia to do the same in reaction to how insane her question is. She knows he would never tell her where to find Brinly but wanted to at least give him one last chance before she sticks him in the deep freeze.

Sophia waits only a moment for the laughter to clear before saying, "I'm going to miss you Ollie. Just know you haven't saved her, only delayed the inevitable. The beast will be mine."

Sophia kisses her finger and places it on his lips before instructing the Jacks to take the Time Broker away as she instructs her agents to relocate Ollie to a secret location quietly tucked away where nobody will find him. …

And just like a breeze in the night Ollie was gone…

Hid from the world for an eternity…

Epilogue

BREAKING NEWS

Several months later…

After taking a very personal interest in the location of the vanished Time Broker a newly skinned Archie has gone from Jack to Jack following the bread crumbs until it lead him to this point. It was so much easier than Archie was use too now that he blends in with the crowd thanks to the help of Dr. Chase and his Syn Skin as he called it.

Archie had his transparent body covered in a material that mimics his invisible skin in everyway in an experiment deemed a success once Archie looked in the mirror and finally saw his face again.

Exactly like Archie remembered in every way except his eyes, Archie's eyes still glow like galaxies swimming in deep black pools.

So Archie's adopted sunglasses.

Sunglasses that are clearly fighting a losing battle against the subzero chill and icy wind sheer that feels like its cutting through you with every gust high up on a cliff face of the largest mountain in the world.

Archie and the bloody and beaten Jack he took captive have to climb to a certain location on the most icy and treacherous side of Mt. Everest. The temperature doesn't seem to bother Archie at all it's like a slight breeze but the Jack is suffering a fate none would wish for as he's slowly freezing to death with every moment exposed to the frigid elements.

The goal is in the twenty eight thousand foot mark of the mountain and they're almost there. At that elevation hid within the rocky cliff face is an entrance to an abandoned werewolf sanctuary repurposed by the Jacks giving merit to the fact that the mysterious sightings of the legendary yeti are more lupine in background than ever suspected before.

Within this repurposed sanctuary is said to be a minimal staff of Jacks stationed there around the clock to protect the tomb of the Time Broker. And Archie's Jack is the relief scheduled to report to the tomb in three days, aren't they going to be in for a surprise.

Archie's excitement for the upcoming chaos followed by finding his friend has caused him to turn a blind eye to the Jack he's tortured and beaten to near death on one occasion during this journey. A true mistake indeed as the Jack purposely steps on top of a special mine placed there by the Jacks and rigged to set off a chain reaction of explosions before stopping in his tracks.

Archie turns to notice the Jack just standing there and warns him of what will happen if he doesn't comply. I think he threatened to kill the Jack's entire family for a hundred years or so ensuring that whatever future may come, his last name wouldn't be in it.

"NO MORE!" the Jack yells having finally found one the many hidden mines hid throughout the path.

"You dare to speak to me in that tone after what you and your stupid little Jacks have done to Ollie and then to Brinly. You're lucky I don't skin you alive bit by bit while forcing you up the rest of this mountain with your muscles exposed." Archie shouts while mentioning what happened when he and Brinly tried to find Ollie together causing him to get lost in the moment…

Archie knew it was an ambitious plan at best, attacking the Jacks oldest and heaviest guarded stronghold in the world in the hopes that Ollie was in there somewhere. But Brinly was distraught and determined to go in with or without Archie. So they went in together.

Only Archie returned to the outside of the ancient prison for monsters…

Lost in the thought that brought Archie to this moment in time in cold blistering snow he only glances back at the Jack for a moment before realizing what his impatience has cost him.

Archie can't even make a move as the Jack he raises his foot allowing the bomb beneath his boot to explode. Blood and body parts paint the snow white path as a low rumble vibrates under Archie's feet.

Instantly this triggers a chain reaction of explosions from the tomb so strong it erases the landscape and causes the already rumbling earth to release an avalanche so massive it buries Archie beneath a hundred feet of ice and rubble near the bottom of the mountain where the avalanche finally stopped. …

Forty years later…

The signature blue and white glow of the TV fills the room mimicking lightning on a dark night when BREAKING NEWS flashes across the screen followed by the reporters detailed account of a true mystery uncovered.

“THE DISCOVERY OF A LIFETIME HAS OCCURRED THIS WEEK THANKS TO THE RECENT INCREASES OF THE CLIMATE ON ONE OF THE MORE TRECHEROUS PATHS ON MT. EVEREST. THE PATH IN QUESTION HAS BEEN OFF LIMITS SINCE THE LATE SEVENTIES DUE TO ALLEGED SAFETY CONCERNSAFTER A FREAK AVALANCHE.

THIS YEAR’S UNPRECEDENTED RISE IN TEMPERTURES HAVE MELTED THE ICE AND SNOW REVEALING A LARGE STONE VAULT DOOR CUT INTO THE CLIFF FACE.

TWO CLIMBERS MADE THE DISCOVERY WHEN ILLEGALLY SCALING THE OFF LIMIT PATH. THEYPOSTED THE PICTURES OF WHAT THEY FOUND FOUR DAYS AGO, BUT ALL ATTEMPTS TO CONTACT THEM HAS ENDED IN FAILURE, AS IF THEY VANISHED OFF THE FACE OF THE PLANET.

IT’S SURE TO SAY THIS IS ‘THE DISCOVERY OF A LIFETIME’ COINED BY ONE GROUP OF ARCHEOLOGISTS WHO HAVESTUDIED THE SYMBOLS COVERING THE MIGHTY STONE DOOR EXTENSIVLY UNSURE OF WHAT THEY MEAN OR HOW THEY’RE GOING TO GET UP THERE TO SEE

WHAT'S BEHIND IT. BUT THEY ARE EXCITED TO FIND OUT, HAVING ALREADY STARTED THEIR LONG TREK UP EVEREST.

AS I UNDERSTAND IT, THEY'RE NOT THE ONLY GROUP SCRAMBLING UP THE MOUNTIAN BEFORE THE ICE AND SNOW CONCEALS THE PATHWAY AGAIN. "...

"Thank you Mother Nature." Archie says out loud to the TV as he realizes what they have uncovered.

Archie's searched the mountain for forty years now looking for his friend Oliver Pendulum covering the most ground in the last few years thanks to the help of a young teleporter named Tinsley as payment for services rendered.

In all his years climbing Everest after the explosions that erased his directions Archie has yet to locate the tomb. He's also yet to give up but those damn Jacks are quite clever.

The Jacks went out of their way to hide the entrance of the tomb of the Time Broker...

But now their TIME...

...Is UP!

The End

.

About the Author

Terry T. Turner, native of Nashville, Tennessee, is thrilled to bring to life this next tale to the masses. Through the years of balancing work with work plus a dash of play added to the mix gives Terry the wild prospective and inquisitive mindset to find a unique way to bring his worlds to life. So thank you for taking the time to read about the goofy guy who writes these truly entertaining tales.

The Chronometer

The Chronometer